MW00532014

"If I d...

write him!

"And I can just imagine what your heroes must be like," Lance retorted. "Rich, suave—"

"Some of them are," Charity broke in.

"—wimps who instantly begin making fools of themselves after falling in love at first sight."

"They're strong, sensitive men who aren't afraid of an honest emotion!"

"Ah, yes," he mocked, "sensitivity—the new measure of a man."

"I wouldn't expect someone like you to understand!"

"Of course not. A real man isn't sensitive enough for a romantic like you!"

"I don't have any trouble with real men. It's twentieth century Neanderthals walking around carrying guns that I can't deal with."

"Is that directed at present company?"

"Are you feeling especially Neanderthal-like today?"

He wanted to say yes, because every time he looked into her bright eyes and saw those sensuous, pouty lips, he felt primal urges...

Dear Reader:

The spirit of the Silhouette Romance Homecoming Celebration lives on as each month we bring you six books by continuing stars!

And we have a galaxy of stars planned for 1988. In the coming months, we're publishing romances by many of your favorite authors such as Annette Broadrick, Sondra Stanford and Brittany Young. Beginning in January, Debbie Macomber has written a trilogy designed to cure any midwinter blues. And that's not all—during the summer, Diana Palmer presents her most engaging heroes and heroines in a trilogy that will be sure to capture your heart.

Your response to these authors and other authors of Silhouette Romances has served as a touchstone for us, and we're pleased to bring you more books with Silhouette's distinctive medley of charm, wit and—above all—romance.

I hope you enjoy this book and the many stories to come. Come home to romance—for always!

Sincerely,

Tara Hughes
Senior Editor
Silhouette Books

GLENDA SANDS

The Man
of Her Dreams

Silhouette *Romance*

Published by Silhouette Books New York

America's Publisher of Contemporary Romance

SILHOUETTE BOOKS
300 E. 42nd St., New York, N.Y. 10017

Copyright © 1988 by Glenda Sands

All rights reserved, including the right to reproduce
this book or portions thereof in any form whatsoever.
For information address Silhouette Books,
300 E. 42nd St., New York, N.Y. 10017

ISBN: 0-373-08565-6

First Silhouette Books printing March 1988

All the characters in this book are fictitious. Any
resemblance to actual persons, living or dead, is
purely coincidental.

SILHOUETTE, SILHOUETTE ROMANCE and colophon
are registered trademarks of the publisher.

America's Publisher of Contemporary Romance

Printed in the U.S.A.

Silhouette Romance

GLENDA SANDS's

feature-writing career led her to cow lots and campaign trails, chimney sweeps and cookie entrepreneurs before she, as she puts it, "stumbled onto the primrose path of fiction." A native Texan, Ms. Sands now lives in Florida with her husband and two children.

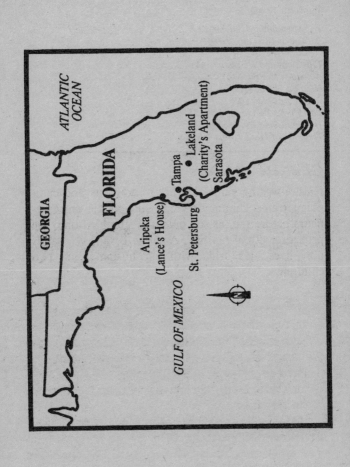

Chapter One

Charity Lovejoy was too preoccupied to notice the breathtaking view of the Gulf of Mexico visible through the window as she stepped out of the elevator. Heavy wool carpet muffled her footsteps in the long corridor as she followed brass-plated signs to the room she was looking for.

Her agent, Tony Tyson, answered her knock promptly, gesturing her into his suite with a wide sweep of his arm. Chuckling at his tropical print shirt, cotton shorts and beach sandals, Charity said, "It didn't take you long to get acclimatized, I see."

Tony shrugged. "When in Rome, do as the Romans. When in Florida..."

"Do as the rest of the tourists," Charity finished for him, with a tinkle of laughter.

"I don't mind looking like a tourist. The snowdrifts were taller than palm trees when I left New York. This is heaven." He aimed a kiss in the general area of her cheek on his way to the bar. "You look gorgeous, as always. What can I get you to drink?"

"Something soft. I want my wits about me when you try to bamboozle me into something I'll regret later." Her eyes quickly surveyed the parlor suite, the view of the surf. "*He* hasn't arrived, I take it."

Tony thrust a glass toward her. "Don't tell me the emerging grand mistress of the sensitive, sizzling sex scene is worried about dealing with a man."

A frown was tugging at Charity's lips as she raised the glass to take a sip. "I don't know whether I spend more time trying to live down that review or live up to it."

"You don't have to do either one, sweetheart. Just be glad you got it. Bad reviews are better than no reviews, and provocative reviews are better yet."

"Let's wait on the royalty statements before we make any judgments."

Tony gestured for her to sit, and she settled into one of the two couches that faced each other in the conversation area. "I'm still not sure about this collaboration, Tony. What was Lance Palmer's attitude when you approached him?"

"I told you, Charity, he's open-minded about it. He's as anxious to break into fiction as you are into mainstream books. You look skeptical. Don't you trust me?"

"I might," she said and hesitated for effect. "But I heard Lance Palmer speak once, and he didn't have good things to say about romance. In fact, on a scale of one to ten, I'd say romance got about a minus twenty in his estimations. So if the man doesn't respect what I do, why would someone with his credentials agree to work with me? There must be other writers you could team him with who could tone down that rough style of his into readable fiction. Why me?''

"I thought you said you'd never met the man," Tony said.

"I didn't meet him, I heard him. He was keynote speaker at that conference in Miami last year, the one where I did the romance workshop. I actually went as far as buying his book, but when he took all the cheap shots at romance in his speech I didn't bother to have it autographed."

"Lance can be blunt . . ."

"And opinionated."

"And opinionated. But underneath he's a pretty likable guy," Tony said. "Once you get to know him—" His thought was cut short by heavy knocking on the door.

Good heavens, Charity thought. *He sounds as though he's about to make a bust. You can take a cop out of uniform, but you can't take the uniform out of a cop.* She stood up and waited for Tony to make the introductions.

Lance Palmer hadn't changed much since Miami, she decided, except that he was wearing slacks and a casual shirt instead of a suit. He was a large man, tall and broad-chested with light brown hair. He exuded an aura of brute strength that made Charity uncomfortable. A sprinkling of interesting scars on his boy-next-door face attested to his years as a street cop. The most prominent of these, a gash parallel to his lower lip, looked as though it might have been acquired in a rowdy free-for-all. He was cordial enough to Tony, but his face showed more skepticism than enthusiasm for the meeting ahead.

"I told you about Charity Lovejoy," Tony said.

Lance extended a hand that completely enveloped hers as he shook it, and his voice was thick with sarcasm. "So this is the emerging grand mistress of the sensitive sizzling sex scene who's going to rescue my work from a hard-boiled style."

Tony leapt in to forestall the scathing retort forming on Charity's lips. "I sent Lance some clips of your reviews. Obviously he read them."

"It would be interesting to know if he's read one of my books," Charity said, meeting Lance's challenging stare head on.

"I wasn't sure I would survive the excitement," Lance said. Charity couldn't tell from his deadpan face and dry delivery whether he was teasing or dead serious. She suspected the latter.

"I read *The Cost of Being a Cop*," she said, smiling up at Lance, wondering if he was astute enough to see through the facade of her sudden sweetness.

"Sit down, children," Tony said. "You know why we're here. We've got business to discuss. I believe you've both made a few notes about your concerns about a possible collaboration."

They sat, Lance on one couch, Charity directly opposite on the other, Tony in the position of referee in an armchair perpendicular to the two. They took out their notes like jousters readying lances, Charity withdrawing a file folder from a chic, businesslike leather portfolio, Lance fishing a pocket-sized spiral-top notebook from his hip pocket. Charity's list was typed in crisp black strokes on quality bond paper. Lance's handwriting, a large, prominent scrawl, was scratched with a felt-tip pen on the standard lined paper of the small notebook.

Charity, being very careful to keep her knees firmly pressed together while she balanced the open file folder in her lap, felt her worst fears about working with Lance Palmer being realized. In every conceivable way, they were different, beginning with the way they approached their work. If Tony had not exacted a promise from her to discuss the possibility of a collaboration with an open mind, she would thrust the file folder back into her portfolio and leave immediately, before all three of them wasted an hour or two coming to the conclusion that was already so obvious to her. Unless her intuitive sensors were malfunctioning, it was just as obvious to Lance Palmer that this particular collaboration was a bad idea.

But she had promised to do this and, undoubtedly, so had Lance Palmer. They had to go through the motions.

A strained silence overcame even the easy-listening music coming from the radio as she and Lance eyed each other speculatively, each waiting for the other to be the first to speak. Tony shifted impatiently in the chair. "Do we do this alphabetically, draw straws or put age before beauty?"

"Ladies first, by all means," Lance said with a mocking condescension that nettled Charity all the way to her bones.

Again, she countered his ill-disguised scorn with a saccharine smile that revealed orthodontically perfect teeth but didn't reach her eyes. She tilted her head toward him dramatically. "I was taught to respect my elders. I bow to age."

Lance clamped his jaw to keep from saying something uncivil. How in the hell had Tony talked him into even considering teaming up with this little snippet?

What kind of woman smiled at you while she was target-sighting you for a verbal grenade launch?

Not Lance's type of woman, that was for sure. He'd been right about Charity Lovejoy in Miami. One brief glimpse of her performance there had been enough to tell him everything he needed to know about her. She was beautiful but cool, cold as ice.

Wishing the meeting were over so they could go home and forget this absurd idea of Tony's, he consulted his notes and said, not bothering with tact, "It would have to be a working partnership. Equal pay for equal work. I don't want someone who's going to go over my manuscript and pretty it up a little and then coast on my track record."

The earlier silence seemed a minor thing in comparison to the pregnant lack of movement and noise that reverberated between them now. Tony would not have stepped between the two couches for fear of being demolished by the hostile energy flashing back and forth between his two favorite clients. Who would have thought two sensible adults would react to each other like flint striking flint? He cleared his throat. "Charity, how do you feel about that?"

Charity read from the neatly typed page, enunciating each word carefully. "Any collaboration would have to be an equal partnership in all aspects, with equal contribution by each partner to creative functions and actual writing." Her eyes flashed with challenge as she lifted them from the paper to glare at Lance. "I would not, under any circumstances, allow myself to be relegated to the role of line editor or clerical worker."

"Sounds to me like you're both saying the same thing here," Tony said. "Lance? Any other concerns?"

"If I'm going to write a novel, it's going to be a novel," he said. "I'm not to gloss over any unpleasantness or stop in the middle of the action for any schmaltzy romantic tripe."

Charity skimmed her list again, deliberately stalling to irritate Lance. "No tacky instant sex or gratuitous violence," she read.

Tony leaned forward in his chair and looked from Lance to Charity. "So you, Lance, don't want too much of what Charity usually does, and Charity, you don't want to go overboard on the violence. Sounds reasonable to me. That's the whole logic in teaming you two up. Ball's back to you, Lance."

"I want to deal with real people. Realistic language, intelligent characters. If we decide to write a book—" Lance said it as though it were a most remote possibility "—we're going to write a damned good one."

"No macho-man-and-the-bimbo story lines," read Charity. "The hero and heroine will be intelligent adults whose talents, qualities and abilities complement each other in the story."

Tony flung his hands in the air. "See? Didn't I tell you this would work?"

Lance and Charity, who had been scowling at each other, turned in unison to direct their scowls at Tony. A comical grin played over his face. "This is good, folks. We have a good dialogue here. Let's keep it going. Lance?"

Lance shifted uncomfortably on the couch. "This isn't about the book, really, but it's something we have to deal with if we're really serious about teaming up."

"By all means get it out on the table," Charity said. "No need to walk on eggs out of respect for my sensibilities."

"It's publicity," Lance said. "I don't mind talking to reporters, but I'm not going to pose for any cheesy publicity photos where we dress up in formal clothes and sit across a candlelit table from each other, or sit on the same beach blanket clinking champagne glasses together so they can write captions like, 'Lance Palmer and Charity Lovejoy plot their new romantic suspense novel.' We play it straight."

For the first time there was genuine amusement in Charity's smile. Consulting her typewritten notes again, she read, "No Bonnie-and-Clyde photos or personal angles in publicity."

"I agree completely," Lance said.

"Stop the presses. It's a modern miracle!" Tony interjected.

Ignoring him, Lance continued, "If this project should progress to the point that we're dealing with publicity, no gimmicks. And nothing personal. No hype about anything but the book."

"Obviously we're clear on the publicity issue," Tony said, "but that's putting the cart before the horse. The question is, is there going to be a book to publicize? Are there any other concerns about a collaboration you want to bring up?" He directed a prompting glare at Lance, who shrugged.

"I've said everything I need to say."

"Charity?" Tony said.

"Same here."

Tony raised his hands. "Well, lady and gent, it's decision time. You both know the situation. Lance, you've got the fame and the fortune, but you want to switch from nonfiction to fiction and your editor's concerned that your style might be a little harsh. And you've never plotted a fiction work, created fictional characters, so you would benefit from having someone walk through the fiction process with you the first time out.''

He turned to Charity. ''You've written seven romances and received good reviews. Now you want to get out of category romance and do a big book. You've got a lovely, lyrical style, and a respectable following, but even so, it's always a gamble breaking into mainstream. If you coauthored a book with Lance here, you'd have a broader readership base when you make the plunge.''

He leaned forward in the chair. ''If you two come up with a book that combines your separate expertises and exploits both your audiences, we could have a big winner on our hands. I have a gut instinct on this: teaming you two is a stroke of genius. It would be a marriage made in heaven.''

''Wrong, Tony,'' Charity said. ''It would be a marriage made in New York. By you and the publisher's publicity department.''

Tony shrugged. ''Heaven. New York. What's the difference? What we're talking here is money and exposure. So what do you say? Will we have a book?''

Charity fixed what she hoped was an interested but noncommittal expression on her face. She was not— absolutely *not*—going to be the first to make a decision. If she agreed to try a collaboration and Lance refused she'd die of humiliation. No, the decision was his. If he was willing to try, she would, too. But only if he committed himself to the project first.

Lance was sitting forward on the couch, absently drumming his fingers together as he thought how ridiculous the entire situation was. Someone had to say something soon, and it looked like he was drafted. Cream puff Lovejoy was sitting there with all the gumption of a decorative pillow waiting for him to take the initiative.

Taking the initiative, he said, "I don't know. It might work in theory, but I'm not convinced there's enough enthusiasm to keep it rolling."

Tony turned to Charity. "What about you, Charity? How's your enthusiasm?"

"I don't know, either, Tony. Like Lance said, it might work, but..."

Tony sprang from the chair unexpectedly. "I think you two might deal with this better if you could talk this out without any pressure from me. So, if you'll excuse me, I'm going poolside and soak up some of your Florida sunshine. When you've reached a decision, hunt me up. We'll have lunch on the terrace."

A wave of panic swept over Charity in the wake of Tony's brisk departure. Lance Palmer had been minimally civil so far, but without Tony to run interference, he might decide to slice her up into manageable portions and have her for lunch instead of waiting for club sandwiches and potato chips on the terrace. What was she doing here trying to talk business with Tampa's version of *Dirty Harry* anyway? How had she ever let Tony talk her into this?

For several terrible seconds it seemed they would just sit there staring at each other, neither knowing what to say or where to begin. Then, abruptly, Lance rose and walked toward the bar. "I could use a drink. How about you?"

Charity glanced at her glass of cola, which was still full, and shook her head. "I'm fine." She felt some of the tension drain from the taut muscles in her neck. *So far, so good.* They'd exchanged a few words and she wasn't bleeding yet.

She heard the sounds of water running, liquid being poured, ice tinkling against glass, muted footsteps on the carpet. Lance sat down opposite her again and took a sip from his glass. Charity might have said something—anything—to chip away at the wall of silence between them, but she couldn't come up with anything to say that wouldn't sound forced or, worse, silly.

After a second draft of his drink, Lance put his glass on the coffee table and looked at Charity as though seeing her for the first time. "You must be Charity Lovejoy. I'm Lance Palmer, your blind date."

The unexpected humor was so delightful that Charity laughed aloud. "It does feel a little like a blind date, doesn't it?"

"I wondered if you could do that."

"Do what?"

"Laugh, and really mean it."

All traces of her laughter faded in response to the note of censure in his voice. "This meeting hasn't exactly been high comedy."

"This meeting hasn't even been low comedy," he agreed. "I suppose Tony coerced and cajoled you into this farce, too."

"Farce is a good word for it."

"Why'd you come?"

"Why did you?"

"What made you think I'd expect you to be a glorified secretary?"

"What made you think I was after a free ride?"

Lance picked up his drink again and, because she had to do *something*, Charity picked hers up, too, and took a sip. Watery cola. Just what she needed. She put the glass back on the table with a soft thud and, catching sight of her hand, examined the nail she'd broken on the car handle that morning.

"Major casualty?" Lance asked sardonically.

"Minor irritation," she snapped back. "If I hadn't forgotten to put an emery board in this purse, I'd file it before the rough edges snag something."

He dug in his pocket, pulled out small clippers. "I think one of the blades has a file side."

"Thanks," she said, taking the clippers and thinking, *The beast has a human side!* The file was rather crude but it got the job done. She twisted the blade back into place and handed the clippers back to Lance.

"Do you think we should try it?" he asked.

"I... Do *you*?"

Lance's hand was massaging the back of his neck again. "Beats me. Tony's convinced it would be good for both of us."

My God! Charity thought. He's as unsure of this whole thing as I am. For the first time it occurred to her that she might be able to tolerate him under the right circumstances. "Tony's got good instincts about this business, especially when he smells money," she said.

"You think it would work, then."

"I think if it did, it would be very exploitable. As for the two of us working together..."

The unfinished thought hung there for several seconds before Lance surprised her by saying, "I don't have anything against making money. Maybe we should try it."

Then Charity surprised herself y replying, "Maybe we should."

"If it didn't work out, we could always say we gave it our best shot."

"The publisher will want an outline and several chapters before we actually sign anything. By the time we have that—"

"We ought to know whether we could work as a team," he finished.

"And if we can't, well, then—"

"Tony can't browbeat us for not trying."

They pondered the prospect individually in their minds. Lance reached for his glass again. "How would we begin?" Charity asked. Lance looked at her, then finished the drink in a single draft.

Liquid courage? Charity wondered. To deal with her? Mr. Macho Ex-cop wasn't as cocksure as he'd like everyone to believe.

He grinned. "My place or yours?"

"You're teasing, I hope."

"We can't work together without meeting somewhere." His grin widened into a totally disarming smile.

Face Lance Palmer on his own turf or let him into the place where she lived and worked—it was like trying to chose between being shipwrecked in rough seas or sucked up by a tornado. The idea of going to his place was intimidating, but then, so was having him wandering through her apartment, sitting at her desk, looking at the pictures on her walls and the magnets on her refrigerator, petting her cat. Perhaps she'd feel more comfortable if she found out more about him before she let him invade her personal niche in the planet. "Your place," she volunteered. "I don't mind driving."

"Good. I'll draw you a map. I'm sort of off the beaten path." She nodded, and he took a deep breath, then exhaled heavily. "We should probably make it as soon as possible."

Grateful for something to do with her hands, Charity opened her portfolio and took out a leather-bound engagement calendar. "Name the day. I mailed off a book last week, so I'm wide open now."

They decided on Wednesday. A nice, neutral day, Charity thought, right in the middle of the week, not too early, not too late. She wrote the particulars in her calendar and closed it, using the map Lance had sketched as a bookmark.

"I've got a few ideas about characters and plots already," Lance said. There was no challenge in his tone, only a presentation of facts.

"So have I," she said, trying to sound equally casual.

"Good." He picked up his empty glass and motioned to Charity's. "Are you finished with this?" She nodded and he carried it to the bar with his own. "I guess characters and a story are the only way to start," he said.

"That's been my experience."

"Charity?" Something about his voice, an element of discomfort, made her turn to look at him. He looked, indeed, rather uncomfortable, as though he wanted to say something and didn't know how to say it. "I'm pretty casual when I work. You don't have to wear a suit. I mean, you can wear..." He sighed in exasperation. "For God's sake, wear something comfortable."

She could have told him that her suit was very comfortable, thank you very much, but some sympathetic instinct stopped her. Instead, she nodded and said, "All right."

Chapter Two

You like my new jeans don't you?'' The sound of Charity's voice made O.J. pause as he rubbed against her calf. Charity bent over and swooped the tomcat into her arms, cradling him belly-up like a baby and scratching his chest the way he loved to be scratched. "You gigolo," she said. "You don't care how many hairs you get on them as long as they're soft, do you?"

O.J. responded by tilting his head back and purring loudly. "Poor thing," Charity cooed. "Just a slave to your carnal needs, aren't you? Well, for your information, I didn't buy faded jeans for your benefit, I bought distressed denims—at an exorbitant price—so that they wouldn't look new, and Lance Palmer wouldn't know I'd bought them especially for today."

O.J.'s purr reached the pitch of a small boat engine and Charity gave him one final flurry of stroking before setting him back on the floor. "Sorry, old boy, I've got to get going. Got to work with Sir Lance-a-lot today, and I wouldn't want to be late."

O.J. resumed his back-and-forth walking, brushing first his whiskers and then his body against her calves, while Charity put the finishing touches on her makeup and brushed her hair. When she had finished, she planted her hands on her waist and, shaking her head, told him, "I suppose I'm going to have to use the clothes brush." O.J., not in the least apologetic, gave her his best aloof-cat expression and mewed indignantly before following her to the dresser. He was a large, battered tabby with numerous scars left over from *duels de l'amour*, which, contrary to his true temperament, made him appear rather ferocious. She called him O.J. because his orange fur was the color of orange juice.

"He said to come casual, but I think a band of cat hairs would be going a bit overboard," she said, vigorously swiping her clothes brush at the hairs that stubbornly clung to the denim. "I'm not trying to impress him, you understand; I just thought I would show him that I can be as casual as the next person. If I have to work with him, I might as well get along with him. What do you think, O.J.—d'you suppose I can deduct the jeans as a business expense on that rationale?"

O.J. cocked his head as though he understood but was utterly bored by her human conversation, then walked off, his bushy tail held upright, proud in spite of its crookedness. *I'd probably get the same reaction from the Internal Revenue Service,* Charity thought as she watched the cat saunter away. She shrugged philosophically. Tax deductible or not, she'd been needing a new pair of jeans. Her old knock arounds were so faded and tattered that she no longer wore them any farther than the mailbox. And while the "distressed" denims had cost more than the indigo-blue variety she usually bought, the extra expense would be well worth the investment if it broke down some of the barriers of awkwardness between her and Lance.

She had chosen a pink crinkled gauze tunic shirt and gathered it at the waist with a colorful braid tie belt. Had it been five degrees warmer or a month later, she would have worn sandals, but she settled for loafers and lightweight socks. Pausing for one last inspectorial glance at herself in the full-length mirror, she was pleased; no one could possibly term the ensemble anything but casual.

She climbed into her car, and with the map to Lance's house clipped to the sun visor, she started out for the coast. An hour later, she was negotiating the network of serpentine back roads that resembled hen scratches on the map. When Lance Palmer decided to move out, he really moved *out*, she thought, taking note of the boxlike fishing huts that dotted the village. Aripeka certainly was antithetical to Tampa, where Lance had worked as a cop.

His house was a nondescript frame structure that resembled all the other huts in its stark simplicity of design. Lance had posted a note on the door that informed her he would be outside in the back, so Charity walked around, glad she was wearing loafers because a heel of any height would have sunk into the sandy soil with every step. There was no fence, but a profusion of pampas grass along either side of the property effectively defined the dimensions of the yard and provided privacy.

Lance was seated on a patio chair with his feet propped on the railing of a wooden deck, reading a book. A large, handsome dog that appeared to be a shepherd mix was curled into a ball at his feet but leapt up as Charity approached. His low, menacing growl made Lance look up from the book. "Hush, Tilly," he said, reaching down to give the dog a reassuring pat. "It's okay, boy."

The dog, obviously unconvinced, sat down but continued to eye Charity warily.

Lance uncrossed his legs, stood up and greeted Charity with a warm good-morning.

Without the reference points of closed walls, Lance's size was not as imposing as it had been in the small hotel suite, and his easy smile did a lot to defuse his brutish intensity. With her writer's observant eye, Charity noted that he was a man fate had intended for wide open spaces. He was sexy in a rugged, frankly sensual way, she grudgingly admitted to herself, though his type would be better suited to historical romances than to the contemporary stories she wrote.

"Would you like a cup of coffee?" he asked.

"I'd love one," she said. "I didn't make coffee this morning."

Lance gestured for her to have a seat and, noting that the dog was sniffing at her feet, said sternly, "Watch your manners, Tilly."

"He probably smells my cat. You say her name's Tilly?" Charity said, tentatively reaching out to pat the dog's head.

"*His* name is Tilly—short for Attila the Hun," Lance answered.

The dog took Charity's friendly gesture as an invitation for some serious attention and offered her his paw for shaking. The soft sound of Charity's laughter followed Lance into the house.

It was amazing, Lance mused, as he poured coffee into a fresh mug then refilled his own, what a change of clothes and scenery could do for a woman. Her shirt was a bit frilly for his tastes, but all in all her outfit was an improvement over those pristine suits she wore.

Watching her pet Tilly and laugh at the dog's antics, he could almost believe that there was a real warm, living, breathing woman buried under that veneer of ice and polish. And she had a cat. It was probably a white, blue-eyed Persian that spent its days curled up on a velvet pillow on her boudoir couch, but a pet of any kind was a good sign there was a heart beating beneath that not-unappealing bosom.

"Cream or sugar?" he called through the window that overlooked the patio.

"Spoonful of sugar," she answered. He stirred it into the coffee and carried both mugs outside. Tilly had progressed to the point of resting his chin on Charity's knee and was regarding her with soulful eyes as she slowly stroked his head.

It was the first time Lance could ever remember feeling envious of his dog. Not liking the emotion or its implications, he set Charity's mug of coffee on the table beside her with a thud. When he got ready to prop his chin on some woman's knee, it wouldn't be on the knee of the emerging mistress of the sensitive, sizzling sex scene! He wasn't dumb enough to try to compete with fictional romantic heroes. This association was strictly business, and that meant hands off everything except the ideas she brought to their work and the discipline she could teach him.

"I like your place," Charity said, picking up the mug. "It's peaceful."

Lance sank into his chair, automatically propped his feet on the railing, took a sip of coffee and sighed his contented agreement. "Sometimes when I sit out here I forget there's a city within a thousand miles."

"There's a hint of brine in the air."

"The gulf's about half a mile away, as the gulls fly. Tilly and I jog over that way sometimes. By the way, when you get tired of Tilly's little con act, you can just nudge him aside."

"He's not bothering me," she said, idly stroking the dog's head with her left hand while she handled the coffee mug in her right. Her hand was smooth and dainty, her flesh pale against the dog's coat, Lance noticed, and noticed, too, that her fingernails were polished a light shade of pink. He took a sip of coffee and concentrated on the flight of a bird that cawed unexpectedly in the distance.

They drank their coffee without talking, but the silence was not strained, which gave Charity a new optimism about their joint project. Perhaps if they could feel this comfortable with each other so soon, a good working rapport was not an unattainable goal. She was aware when Lance pushed his mug aside but took a few extra minutes to finish her own coffee, then stared at the residue in the bottom of the mug for a few seconds before setting it on the table next to Lance's.

Apparently Lance sensed her change of attitude, her preparedness to get on with business, because he shifted in his chair and exhaled a noncommittal sigh. "What did you think of *The Cost of Being a Cop*?" he asked without preamble.

So much for an easy rapport, Charity thought, feeling the muscles in her neck tense.

"You're stalling," he prompted after a reasonable lapse of silence. "Why?"

"I don't know how you want me to answer."

"The question was simple enough. You told me you read it, I asked what you thought of it."

But do you really want to know? As a writer, Charity knew how vulnerable writers were, that they walked a tightrope between believing their work was good and needing constant reassurance that it was. It took courage to show thoughts that came from inside you to other people, more courage to ask for an opinion. Some writers, when they seemed to be asking for objectivity, really wanted reassurance. She knew what Lance was used to hearing about *The Cost of Being a Cop*, and she wondered if he simply expected to hear more of the same or if he was ready for a more critical opinion.

"You were quick to volunteer that you'd read it; don't you have the guts to tell me what you thought of it?"

Guts, huh? Charity thought, disgusted. Of course a man like Lance would view everything in terms of guts. It was machismo, cop mentality. Well, she thought, squaring her shoulders, I've got the guts to tell you. Let's see if you have the guts—or the grace—to take it.

"I didn't like it at first," she said. "The way it opened on the street with Larry being shot was so graphic. The blood, his screaming, the stark violence of the details. It was powerful, you understand, but it wasn't the type of reading that appeals to me."

"I guess not," he said, the disdain audible in his voice. "It wasn't one of your romantic fantasies where everyone falls in love and lives happily ever after."

"No. But then, it wasn't supposed to be, was it? Just as my books are not supposed to be true crime works.

At least I had the *guts*—'' she stressed the word guts, loading it with disgust ''—to read your book before I ventured an opinion about it. I didn't condemn it through association and prejudice because I was afraid I might find something in it to praise.''

A chortle of incredulous laughter bubbled up from his throat. ''You think I'm *afraid* to read your work?''

''Worse!'' she said. ''You don't think it would be worth your time. You made it perfectly clear what you think about romance novels in your speech in Miami.''

''So that's what's in your craw! A few general comments about genre fiction...''

''Ha!''

He looked at her, surprised by the intensity of her sarcasm, and inhaled sharply. ''You did your share of perpetuating myths about romance writers at that conference.''

Her head jerked around to face him. ''Me?'' She hadn't known he was even aware she was there, that she had been on the staff teaching a workshop while he was the keynote speaker.

''Yes, you, Ms. Lovejoy. The woman in the book room told me you'd bought a copy of *The Cost of Being a Cop*, so when I happened to be passing the room where you were doing your workshop, I slipped in, thinking I'd hang around afterward, introduce myself, offer to sign the book. You know, just say hello.'' His laughter had an unpleasant quality in it. ''I walked in just in time to catch your little performance during the question-and-answer period.''

''Performance?'' she muttered, genuinely puzzled. She didn't remember anything unusual happening at the Miami workshop.

"You know, where you tossed your mane of raven-black hair away from your face like one of your heroines and said, 'I wouldn't want to do anything to my heroines that I wouldn't enjoy myself.'"

She couldn't stop the half laugh that sprang from her throat. "You mean when they asked if I researched my love scenes personally? What was I supposed to say? They weren't expecting a bibliography."

"No," he said smugly. "They weren't. And you didn't disappoint them, did you?"

"That idiotic question is an occupational hazard for romance writers. It comes up in every question-and-answer session." She crossed her arms over her waist and sighed. "The married writers all say something about their husbands being their chief assistant researcher, but since I don't have a husband, I have to handle it with humor."

She turned away from him, looking out over the yard and the trees beyond, wishing she could see the gulf and be calmed by its constancy. "What do you do if they ask if you ever had to kill a man while you were a cop?"

She heard his sharp intake of breath and knew she'd hit a nerve. She turned to face him, but found no satisfaction in the misery that haunted his voice as he replied, "I tell them I'm there to discuss my book, not my record as a police officer."

Enough, she thought. If they were going to work together, this constant nettling of each other was silly and counterproductive. "Are you still interested in what I thought of *The Cost of Being a Cop*?" she asked impatiently.

"I thought you'd told me," he replied sourly.

"Just my first impression, and then we got sidetracked. There's more, if you'd care to hear it."

"By all means, elucidate."

"Another thing that bothered me about your book was the writing. It was very uneven, unpolished. The writer in me was outraged. I couldn't understand why a publisher would let it get into print when it was still a draft away from being good writing. I work so hard to make sure that my work is as good as it can be, and I know so many others who do, that I was offended yours would be just one step above mediocrity and not only get published, but create such a brouhaha and win prizes."

"Should I dig out my bulletproof vest for the next volley?" he asked.

She smiled at him, appreciative of the humor, even if it was caustic. "That won't be necessary. You see, when I kept on reading, I soon realized that the editor had purposely left the rough edges so that the story would be in your voice. It was more effective that way, like sitting down with a cop and hearing it firsthand instead of having it reported on the evening news. And, though I still don't like violence and tragedy, I was drawn into the stories you told. When Charlie went to tell Larry's widow that he was dead, and then later in the book, when Charlie's marriage broke up, I began to see the genius, and a certain sensitivity behind the power. I cried when Charlie went to see his baby and his ex-wife told him she was getting married again and asked him to let her new husband adopt his child."

She swallowed. Discussing the stories he'd told had recalled the empathy she'd felt when first reading them. "The other stories were just as touching, even though they were…ugly. Pete becoming an alcoholic and dying of liver disease, Marcie having to have a hysterectomy after she was kicked in the stomach by a junkie, Joe having to resign from the force after the shooting incident.''

There were tears in her eyes. Lance would have sworn it, even though she blinked them away and would have denied it. He fought an insane urge to draw her into his arms and comfort her as she turned those limpid brown eyes toward him and said, "You've got a gift, Lance. You recognized the stories and told them in a way that even the most devoted ostrich couldn't ignore. If you can bring the same sensitivity, the same intensity, to fiction that you brought to *The Cost of Being a Cop*—"

She paused to catch her breath. "Your talent transcended style in *Cop*, but . . .''

"I have the distinct feeling we've reached the bottom line," Lance said, when she hesitated.

"Talent isn't going to exempt you from working on your style. *Cop* was a once-in-a-lifetime work. You won't get away with writing it over and over and expect the public to keep buying it. You've got to let your skills grow into your talent.''

An awkward silence crept between them as they sat staring at each other, and the suspense of waiting for Lance's reaction made Charity's throat dry.

"Isn't that what you're here for?" he asked finally. When she didn't reply, he said, "Did you think I agreed to this collaboration because of those big chocolate eyes and that sweet little behind of yours?''

"I . . . no!" she said, making up in indignation what she lacked in elegance. "That possibility never even crossed my mind.''

There was a disconcerting tinge of smug satisfaction in his grin. "I guess maybe it didn't.''

Charity was sure there was a slur inherent in the remark, but she had the good sense to bite the inside of her lip to keep from countering with some impulsive, half-baked reply. *You can still back out of this,* she reminded herself.

The last thing she expected was for him to touch her, but he reached out and curled his fingers around the top of her arm and said, "What I meant was, it's obvious you approach writing from a strictly professional perspective."

"That wasn't what you implied a few minutes ago with that crack about my performance at the conference."

Damn! he thought, more affected by the stricken expression in her eyes than he wanted to be. "I was wrong, all right? If I offended you, I'm sorry."

She shrugged her shoulder out of his grasp, and he groaned in frustration. "Damn it, Charity, I agreed to this collaboration because I knew I needed help, and Tony seemed to think you're the one who could give it to me." He drew in a sharp breath. "After what you just told me about *The Cost of Being a Cop*, I'm convinced he's right."

She turned her head slowly to face him. "You are?"

"If you'd batted your eyelashes at me and told me how perfect *Cop* was, I'd have called the entire deal off."

"You were testing me?"

Lance was more intrigued than intimidated by the cold glare she fixed on him. "Not exactly," he said. "I just . . . really, I was just curious whether you'd be open with me."

"You were testing me."

"I found out what I needed to know."

Her eyes narrowed. "You're really into honesty and openness among partners, aren't you?"

He shrugged. "My training, I guess."

"Well, Mr. Ex-cop," she said, poking her index finger into his chest with surprising force, "I'm going to be honest and open with you. We're collaborating on a book, not thwarting crime. You try any more of these little tests of faith on me, this partnership is off. We may not be dealing in life or death here, but we are dealing in careers, and it's almost the same thing. Either you trust my integrity and respect my ability—" she emphasized the point with another savage jab of the finger "—or this partnership is off as of right now."

And an interesting partnership it's going to be, thought Lance as he caught her hand in his. "It's on," he said flatly, casually tossing her hand aside as he let go of it.

For a fleeting expanse of time, perhaps not even a full second, Charity was possessed by the insane idea that he might try to kiss her to seal the pact. Then she had an even more insane thought—she wished that he would. But Lance got up and strolled to the railing of the deck and stared out into the distance as though he, too, longed for the soothing effect of the rolling gulf that was just out of sight, and she was left staring at his back, thinking how broad and powerful his shoulders were.

Don't do it, she warned herself, *don't let his blatant masculinity get to you.*

When Lance turned around, he behaved as though the heated exchange had never taken place. "Shall we work out here, or would you prefer to go inside?"

"Let's stay out here," she said. Inside, he would seem even larger, even more masculine.

He settled back into the patio chair beside her and looked at her expectantly. "You're the old pro. Where do we begin?"

Charity opened her portfolio and took out a notebook. "I think we should decide what kind of story we want to write. Suspense or mystery with two major characters who become romantically involved leaves a pretty wide scope. Any ideas?"

"I'm not real big on spies," he said.

"Good. We agree on something, at least. Don't you have any notes?"

"I don't usually write stuff down."

"You should," she said, holding up the loose-leaf binder. "This is my idea book. I allot a couple of pages for each story idea and write down details as they come to me, and when I wonder what to do next, I flip through it."

Lance's expression was skeptical. "What does it say about a suspense or mystery with two protagonists who become romantically involved?"

She read: "Murder? Madcap caper? Hostage? Kidnapping or abduction? Quest?"

"I thought we'd just start with a body, and bring in a homicide detective and some woman . . ."

"A dumb blonde, no doubt."

Frowning at her interruption, he continued, "Who has some connection to the victim, or maybe who's an unwitting witness . . ."

"Who keeps getting underfoot and keeps the cop from solving the crime?"

"Sort of."

"Where's your imagination, Lance? This isn't episode thirty-nine of some TV cop series. We can't write a hundred-thousand-word cliché! We have to write something original.''

Miffed, Lance said, ''What did *you* have in mind?''

''A madcap caper. Murder is for the mystery purists. We're after a broader audience. Kidnapping or a hostage is okay, but its very confining. If one or both of the main characters is kidnapped, there's no range for mobility. And quest—I don't know. I'm just not much on treasure hunts and yellowing maps that are suddenly hot items after two hundred years.''

''Another point of agreement—about the treasure. I still think we ought to consider a juicy murder, though.''

''We'll probably have to work one into the plot sooner or later to keep up the suspense. But I don't think it should be too close to our protagonists. It can be sort of a peripheral threat.''

''Suppose we do a caper—what are our characters stealing?''

''Or what gets stolen from them? Anything to set them on a merry chase,'' Charity said.

''If we make one of them a cop, it can be anything illegal—a cache of drugs, a smoking gun, plates for counterfeiting. Then all we have to do is get the other character involved.'' She was shaking her head, and he said, irritably, ''What?''

''I don't think either of our main characters should be a cop.''

''One of them has to be.''

She shook her head again.

''I'm not chauvinistic,'' he said, thinking himself quite magnanimous. ''We could have a lady cop.''

Her face remained impassive as she shook her head again.

Lance sniffed in exasperation and said, "How the hell are we supposed to get them involved in some caper then?"

"That's why they call it creative writing, Palmer."

"It's logical to make one of them a cop," he said, crossing his arms over his chest and setting his jaw in a stubborn clinch.

"It's also very limiting," Charity said. "Cops have to work within a certain framework, follow certain rules...."

"You live in a dream world, lady."

"Maybe in real life they don't. Maybe real cops ignore Miranda and take a few satisfying swipes when they're making an arrest and get away with it. That doesn't mean we can have a fictional detective running roughshod over the Constitution and expect our readers to accept him as a heroic figure."

"It's done all the time."

"Not by me, it isn't! If I don't believe in a character, I don't write him!"

"And I can just imagine what your characters must be like. Rich, suave—"

"Some of them are."

"—wimps who instantly begin making fools of themselves after falling in love at first sight."

"They're strong, sensitive men who aren't afraid of an honest emotion!"

"Ah, yes," he mocked, "sensitivity—the new measure of a man."

"I wouldn't expect a man like you to understand!"

"Of course not. A real man isn't sensitive enough for a romantic like you! It takes a trumped-up hero, taken straight out of round-table armor and electronically zapped into a BMW with his code of chivalry intact."

"I don't have any trouble with real men, Palmer. It's twentieth-century Neanderthals walking around carrying guns that I can't deal with."

"Is that directed at present company?"

"Are you feeling especially Neanderthal-like today?"

He wanted to say that yes, dammit, he was. Every time he looked into her bright eyes and saw those sensuous, pouty lips, he was feeling primal urges. At the moment he found the idea of giving Charity Lovejoy a good rap on the head very appealing.

"The world would certainly be simpler," he said, "if we went back to the system of males conking females on the head and dragging them off."

"I can't believe even you would say that!" she said, though she wasn't surprised at all, merely mildly irritated. And strangely fascinated by the mental image of Lance Palmer dragging a female behind him by the hair—especially since the hair she saw him using for a handle was the exact rich shade of brunette as her own.

"At least the old tribal conk was honest and straightforward. It's hearts-and-flowers romance that's mucked up male and female relations. Mating was uncomplicated before marriage licenses and mortgages. There wasn't a one-in-three divorce rate, either."

Charity sniffed exasperatedly. "There wasn't a divorce rate at all. Women just lived with what men dished out until one or the other of them got gobbled up by some carnivore, which usually didn't take long. If a woman was smart, she probably left a trail of animal fat so the predators could find the clod easily."

"Tut, tut, Ms. Lovejoy. Let's not go putting twentieth-century barbarism in the mind of Neanderthal women. Something has to be sacred."

"Meaning the myth of a mindless, totally submissive female who enjoyed being conked on the head?"

"Meaning a female who was woman enough to enjoy being in the cave once she got there."

Charity felt the sting of insult, though she could not pinpoint exactly how he had managed to impregnate the comment with a personal connotation. Squaring her shoulders, she said, rather sharply, "We're off the subject."

But this is so much fun, Lance thought. Still, reluctantly, he accepted the fact that they had to get back to work. "You were opining, I believe, that we should not make either of our protagonists a cop."

"Because it's too limiting," she said, relieved they were back to business. "He'd have to stick to too many rules and, should there be a sequel, or if we turned these into series characters...." She froze as his gaze caught hers and the implication of their characters turning into series characters and a single collaboration turning into a long-term partnership skittered between them. "We'd always be limited to the same rules and thinking in terms of cases," she finished lamely, feeling an irrational blush spread over her face.

"In other words, cops are boring." He was baiting her on purpose, turning her words against her. And thoroughly enjoying himself. He forced his face into a serious mask as he watched her steel herself before answering.

"As series characters in mainstream novels, yes," she said curtly.

His responding silence was more effective than anything he could have said, leaving her wondering if she had, in fact, hurt his feelings. When the silence became protracted, she said, "I didn't mean it personally. I don't have anything against cops. It's just that ..."

She frowned in response to the stoic expression on his face. "Dammit, you were a cop. Wasn't a lot of your work routine, despite the high points and the glory moments?"

Lance exhaled heavily. Had there been high points, glory moments? Like when he'd arrested fifteen-year-old Carlos Ramos? Or shot seventeen-year-old Mike Travis? All those glorious moments that had sent him home to collapse on the sofa and bury his face in his hands and wonder why being one of the good guys didn't feel good? The high points that had sent Katy storming out in a rage and ended their marriage! "Yeah," he said. "A lot of it was pretty routine."

"I think we should steer away from private investigators, too."

"No argument. I never wasted any love on the freelance boys. I don't know why I would want to write about one."

They became lost in their individual thoughts for a moment, and then Charity, digging in her portfolio, said, "Why don't we approach this from a different angle. Let's get our characters pinned down and then we can work on the story line." She opened the manila file folder she'd just located and looked down at the printed forms inside. "I have a form I've made up that helps me get in touch with my characters."

The idea of getting in touch with fictional characters brought an amused grin to Lance's face, although he stopped himself from asking her if she felt like a medium. "You're pretty organized, aren't you?"

"Insurance companies file policies, banks file accounts—why shouldn't a writer organize ideas?" He was staring at her with a skeptical expression on his face; she licked her lips nervously before continuing, "When you're blocked, a familiar routine can get the creative juices flowing again. Organization is always more productive than chaos."

Whatever Lance had thought of Charity Lovejoy before that moment, it was not that she was cute. But she was. He suddenly couldn't comprehend why he hadn't noticed the slight upward tilt that saved her nose from patrician perfection, or the sprinkling of freckles the light makeup she wore didn't quite hide, or the wisps of hair that coiled in ringlets near her hairline.

He knew enough about women to know she probably hated those uncontrollable tendrils, and enough about Charity to realize she would despise anything she couldn't control or organize to the nth degree. Personally, he liked those rebellious, wispy little curls, the tilt of her nose, the freckles she tried to hide. He was even beginning to like Charity Lovejoy. And he was beginning to wonder what those sensuous lips would taste like if he kissed her—wonder if he dare try to find out.

Deciding the entire idea of trying was insane—not to mention downright impractical—he shifted in the chair, lowering his feet from the railing to the floor as though drawing himself to attention as he forced his mind back on business. "Let's see this magic form."

"There's nothing hocus-pocus about it," Charity said, as she leaned in the direction of Lance's chair, holding the sheet so he could read it. "It's just a guide to make you think about the person you want to create."

He chuckled. "What's this about ice-cream cones?"

"Don't laugh, Lance. You can tell a lot about a person's personality by thinking about what kind of ice cream he'd order at Baskin-Robbins. You know, people who order vanilla aren't very creative, but it would take a frivolous adult to order bubble gum.''

His grin was almost endearing. "What about double-Dutch chocolate?"

"Ah!" she said. "A purist with a no-nonsense approach to decision making. He's not out to impress anyone because he doesn't feel like he has to."

Without commenting, Lance looked back at the paper. "You really sit around and try to figure out what a person would have in his wallet or purse?"

"You can tell a lot about the person's economic and social position by which credit cards he has or how much cash he carries. And the business cards: appointment cards for the doctor, the dentist or the hair stylist, whether the appointments are in the future or the cards are out of date. Women carry mirrors and makeup, or mace, or disposable diapers, or good-luck tokens. Photographs or old ticket stubs show sentimentality. Knives or guns..."

"All right, all right," he said, raising his hand to forestall her lecture. "I get the point. I guess since I wrote about people I knew personally, I didn't realize how difficult it would be to make fictional characters seem real." He continued skimming the form again. "What's this about the refrigerator and the pantry?"

"It's very revealing."

"I don't believe it."

With a light of mischief in her eyes, Charity stood up. "Come on, Palmer, I'll prove that reading a refrigerator is as telling as reading a palm."

It was an obvious dare, and Lance knew he had no choice about following her into his kitchen and watching as she rummaged through the sacred, private place inside the insulated walls of his refrigerator. She seemed to be thoroughly enjoying herself, which irritated him, and the fact that she was managing to irritate him irritated him even more.

Resting his hand on the top corner of the open refrigerator door, he was less than a foot away from her as she plunged her head and shoulders into the task of analyzing the assemblage of jars and deli wrappers.

"Lunch meat, cheese, mustard, no mayonnaise," she said. "You make sandwiches for yourself, but not for anyone else." Wrinkling her nose at the contents of a wadded piece of waxed paper, she held it at arm's length. "Sometimes you buy food and don't get around to finishing it." The nauseating odor of advanced decay wafted through the air. "My God, Palmer, what *was* that?"

Relieving her of the noxious bundle, he consulted the torn deli label before depositing the entire parcel in the garbage pail. "Pastrami," he announced solemnly.

She lifted another wad of the same type of paper, cautiously peeped inside and said, "I think this is the cheese that went with it." She surrendered it to him with a sigh of relief and heard it land in the trash can with a thud. "It wasn't Limberger by any chance?" she asked hopefully.

"Uh-uh," he said, shaking his head.

"I was afraid not," she said. "You know, I'll bet the salmonella count in this refrigerator is high enough to contaminate an entire city's food supply."

"Salmonella?" he said.

"Don't ask. You'll probably have a close encounter with it eventually, and I wouldn't want to scare you." Reasserting herself to the task at hand, which she now regarded as hazardous duty, she opened the meat drawer. "Aha! Bacon with a future sell-by date! That's encouraging. Added to the relatively fresh eggs and the jelly on the door, I'd say you're a definite breakfast person."

The vegetable crisper held a mixture of the bad, the beautiful and the downright disgusting. "Was this apple from last year's growing season?" Charity asked, holding the plastic produce bag by the corner, so that the moldy lump inside dangled in front of Lance's face like a pendulum.

He relieved her of it with a terse, "It's a pear, actually."

"*Was* a pear," Charity corrected. She continued foraging. "These radishes are gorgeous. And the lettuce and green onions are in pretty good shape. The cucumbers are marginal." Closing the drawer, she straightened up. "I'd say either you hate to cook or you're health-conscious enough to eat a lot of salads. Quite probably a combination of the two."

She had not realized how close together they were until she stood up straight and turned, only to come nose to knit with the fabric of his shirt where it stretched across his chest. After having been in the cold refrigerator up to her waist, she was immediately conscious of the warmth of his body just inches from hers and, when their eyes met, the light, airy smile that had been forming on her lips evolved into a slightly surprised gasp as she felt an unexpected surge of sexual awareness.

But I don't like brawny men, she protested silently—although the portion of her brain controlling libidinous energy didn't seem to be paying attention. Abruptly, she twisted around and reached for the handle on the freezer door so he wouldn't notice the blush she felt creeping over her cheeks.

"Do we have to go on with this?" he asked impatiently.

"Why stop in the middle?" she said, wondering if he heard the note of artificial flippancy in her voice. She didn't give a damn what was in the freezer as long as digging through it gave her a chance to recover her equilibrium before she had to face those probing eyes of his again. She welcomed the blast of frosty air that swooshed over her as she pulled the door open.

An ice maker took up half the space inside. Several gourmet-style frozen dinners, a couple of French bread pizzas and a Baskin-Robbins ice-cream carton filled the rest. Charity picked up the ice cream, removed the lid, peered inside and cocked her head toward Lance with a "gotcha" grin. "Double-Dutch chocolate, I presume."

"Guilty," he confessed.

Color crept charmingly over his face, and Charity fought against the fresh disarming surge of sexual awareness rising in her in response to the unexpected show of shyness. "Now that I know all your deep, dark secrets," she said, brushing past him and walking in long strides toward the door, "we might as well get back to work."

Chapter Three

Back on the deck, Lance picked up the character-information form and a felt-tip pen. "Might as well start with the heroine," he said, then read, "Hair color?"

"Anything but blond," Charity said.

"But blondes are sexy."

"Especially the dumb ones," Charity parried evenly. "What you do with blondes is between you and the blondes, Palmer, just don't ask me to write a romantic adventure about one. The urge to let her giggle her way through the book would be too irresistible."

"Do brunettes ever giggle?"

"Never," she said.

Lance snorted skeptically and said, "Then let's make her a redhead. We don't want to end up with a rewrite of Anna Karenina."

"Rich auburn and sleek, or strawberry and curly?"

"Strawberry and curly," he said, writing the words as he spoke. "Height?"

"I'm not choosy. Average."

"Five feet, six inches," he said. "Ah! This sounds interesting. Other distinguishing physical characteristics."

"That could be anything—scars, dimples, violet eyes, a limp, freckles...."

"Thirty-six D," Lance said, etching the numbers and the capital letter in his heavy scrawl.

"Tony said a male viewpoint would add a new dimension to my work," Charity said dryly. "I didn't know it would be thirty-six D."

"Don't give me all the credit," Lance countered in the same level tone. "I'd say you got halfway there all by yourself."

Involuntarily, she followed his intense gaze to her chest. Feeling the blush creep over her cheeks, she clenched her jaw and silently counted to ten to keep from saying something she would regret later. How dare he stare at her like that and say such a thing! Halfway there. *Halfway* there! She might not be top-heavy, but she'd never had to resort to powder puffs or old socks to fill out her blouses. Just wait until they worked on the hero!

"Occupation?" Lance read.

Biting back the urge to suggest they take advantage of their heroine's obvious talent and make her a topless dancer, Charity took a deep breath and forced her voice to sound normal. "Let's hold off on that until we see what fits the story line. I see her as a professional, though."

"Oh, yes," he agreed, too quickly. "A pro. Definitely."

"I was referring to one of the newer professions," Charity countered in clipped tones.

Lance lifted his shoulder in feigned innocence. "Would I imply otherwise?"

"Certainly not," Charity said, letting the words drip with sarcasm.

"What, pray tell, does our curly-haired carrot top carry in her purse?" Lance asked, after a cursory glance at the form. "I'm dying with anticipation."

"Would you be serious, please?"

"I am serious. It's always amazed me what women carry in their purses. We used to inventory the contents of their purses when we booked them. Everything from chocolate peanuts to brass knuckles. I swear, one woman had a jar of formaldehyde with her appendix in it. Fought like the dickens to get us to let her keep it. Said she never went anywhere without it."

"*That* doesn't sound like our heroine."

"She didn't look like our heroine, either. She was walking a duck on a leash down the center esplanade of the interstate when we picked her up for public drunkenness and creating a public nuisance."

"She had a duck on the freeway?"

"Um-hum. And the scarf tied around the duck's neck was the only stitch of clothes either of them had on."

"Is that a true story?" she asked incredulously.

Lance raised his hands in the air. "Would I make up something like that? She had her duck on a leash and her purse on her arm, and she was naked as a jaybird and drunk as a skunk. And she raised holy hell when we took her appendix away from her."

"Good grief."

"I've thought about writing *The Funny Side of Law Enforcement* as a companion to *The Cost of Being a Cop*."

"Why haven't you?" Charity asked.

Lance leaned forward, propping his elbows on his thighs and resting his chin on his fists. Charity sensed his withdrawal as he stared into the distance and considered his answer. After a long pause, he raised his head and turned to look at her. "Aside from possible lawsuits, I think the works would be too far apart, too different. It would be like following concrete with feathers."

"Maybe someday," Charity said. She spoke softly, sensitive to his sudden change in mood.

Lance sat up and heaved a sigh. "Maybe. After enough time has passed so people aren't expecting another *Cost of Being a Cop*." He stared into the distance again, and kept staring out as he said, "It's scary, you know. After *Cop*, everyone's expecting so much."

"Everyone feels that way after the first book," she said lightly, touched by his unexpected show of vulnerability. "Competing with yourself is the worst type of competition."

Slowly, he turned his head to look her full in the face. "I might take you with me if I fall on my face."

Meeting his gaze straight on, she smiled. "Then we'll just have to write a damned good book, because I have no intention of falling on my face or my fanny any time soon."

He returned her smile gratefully. "Where did you ever get a name like Charity Lovejoy?"

"I was born with the Lovejoy part. Daughter of Reverend and Mrs. Mark Thomas Lovejoy. The Charity part is a legacy from my grandmother, who was the daughter of a country preacher who named his first three girls Hope, Faith and Charity. My folks named me Charity Anne, and called me Annie until I turned twelve and decided that Charity, however old-fashioned, was more distinctive. It means love, and being Love Lovejoy appealed to my adolescent sense of drama." This time, her smile was self-deprecating. "I seem to recall thinking it was terribly sexy."

Lance said lightly, "Is it true what they say about preachers' kids being wilder than regular kids to show that they're not goody-goodies?"

Charity laughed. "Except for my secret yearning to be the sexiest girl in the sixth grade, I left the hell-raising to my big brother, Steven. He succeeded in tarnishing the goody-goody image for both of us. He got arrested once for soaping a fountain."

Lance exaggerated a gasp. "You mean, you're related to *that* Steven Lovejoy?"

"Sounds silly now, but it was a big deal at the time. My father was furious, my mother was hysterical, and Steven was scared to death, and I was scared to death for him. The charges were dropped after he and his friends agreed to clean the fountain once a week all summer, but Steven still can't stand cops."

"And Steven's little sister isn't too fond of them."

She answered the challenge in his tone with a long, even stare. "I've never had any dealings with any...until now."

After a long silence, she asked, "Why did you quit?" He didn't answer, and she said, "Was it just the burning desire to write full time?"

"No," he said, the word coming in a gush of air that betrayed strong emotion. "It was more than that."

He obviously didn't want to talk about it, and Charity decided to let him off the hook. "Well, you're a writer now," she said, "and if you don't want to starve next year, we'd better get back to work. Let's shelve the heroine's purse until we decide what her occupation is and think about the hero for a while."

She picked up a pen and took out a blank form. "Name. Let's hold off on that until we decide what he does for a living."

"Works for me," Lance agreed.

"Hair color?"

The light-brown-haired Lance shrugged, and Charity, seeing the perfect opportunity to get even with him for their busty heroine, said, "I think he should have jet-black hair. Dark men are so virile."

She gave the last word a sensuous inflection that Lance would have had to have been deaf to miss. He clenched his jaw momentarily before saying, "Black hair, then."

"Height," Charity read and, before Lance could reply, said, "Let's make him just under six feet. Tall men—really tall men—tend to have egos to match their size. We wouldn't want our heroine to get a crick in her neck if she goes dancing with him."

Lance, easily six-foot three, shrugged his shoulders. "Whatever you say."

"Other distinguishing physical characteristics. Let's make him very lean. Lean men look so sleek in a suit."

"Fine," Lance grumbled.

"Beefy men are so . . . beefy."

"You've made your point," said Lance-of-the-broad-chest-and-bulging-biceps, and then, looking at Charity, grumbled exasperatedly, "I thought you said brunettes never giggled."

"Only if provoked," she said. "I swear, Lance, your expression was priceless."

After a tense pause, he burst out laughing, and she laughed again, really laughed rather than giggled. "You deserved it, you know."

"I suppose so," he admitted, and, picking up the character form, said, "We're back to occupation."

"Which brings us back to needing a basic story line before we get any further with our characters," Charity agreed.

Unexpectedly, Lance stood up. "I'm not used to sitting around while I'm trying to think." He glanced at the no-frills diver's watch on his wrist. "It's almost one. I was planning on heating up those frozen dinners for lunch, but I wonder..."

Charity cocked an eyebrow to indicate she was still listening. Lance raised his right hand to massage the muscles in his neck. "I could use some exercise. There's a sandwich shop about half a mile from here that serves great hoagies and homemade soup. How would you feel about a walk?"

"I'd love a walk," she said. Lifting a foot into the air, she pointed to her well-worn loafer. "I even seem to have come prepared."

"If I walk too fast, just tell me to slow down," Lance said as they reached the end of the driveway and turned onto the road.

"I'll do my best to keep up," Charity said dryly, and being a frequent and enthusiastic walker, she did a respectable job of maintaining the brisk pace Lance set.

"Tony talked you into this collaboration, didn't he?" Lance asked after a long but comfortable silence.

"Tony has a way of being very persuasive," Charity said without breaking stride. "How about you?"

"Dragged into it kicking and screaming," he admitted.

"Why did you agree to it?" she asked, casting him a sideways glance.

Lance slowed his pace perceptibly. "He said although I'd had a hotshot best-seller, it was a Cinderella book and I had a lot to learn." His eyes met hers. "He says you're a good writer, and that you teach writing as well as write."

"I used to teach high-school English. Now I'm down to one class per semester at the community college," she said. Then, "Just how much kicking and screaming did you do?"

"A lot."

"Why?"

He didn't answer immediately. "I'm something of a loner, I guess."

Hearing the evasion in his voice, Charity frowned. So their new easy rapport was a little shaky. She didn't want to argue with Lance, but she wasn't going to let him get away with such vagueness after he'd introduced the area of conflict between them. He'd been the one to fling it between them and now he was dancing around it; irritated, she decided to force the inevitable confrontation and either deal with the issue or call off the entire project. "It's because of my books," she challenged. "The type of books I've written."

"Yes," he said, unflinching.

So much for hemming and hawing, Charity thought. It was going to be a clean, direct confrontation. Part of her—the professional, civilized part—was glad. The rest of her—the strictly human side, she supposed—would have preferred an old-fashioned no-holds-barred, knock down, drag-out fight to a tense, civilized discussion.

"Have you read any of my books?" she asked.

She could almost feel the invisible cloak of defensiveness he wound around himself. "The back-cover copy. The inside teaser."

"But you haven't read one cover to cover, the way I read *Cop*?"

"No," he admitted, in a tone he might use to accuse her of something illicit.

"So you're condemning it through prejudice, without giving it an objective evaluation. Why?"

"Tony said you're a good writer. I took his word for it."

"That's a cop-out." She might have found the ironic humor in the unintentional pun if his attitude hadn't infuriated her so.

For almost a minute they walked even faster than before. Charity was nearly running in order to keep up with him, but she was grateful for the exertion. The tension between them was almost tangible as she waited for him to return the volley.

Finally, as oppressed by the tense silence as she, he said, "I don't care for romance."

"Pardon me if I don't burst into tears at the slight," she said, "but I happened to catch *your* performance in Miami, and I realize it's nothing personal. It's not just my books you're condemning sight unseen, it's all romance novels. What I can't figure out is why you went into partnership with someone you clearly don't respect."

He stopped, planted his feet side by side on the asphalt and, reaching out to encircle her forearm, forced her to stop as well. "I respect you, okay?"

"You don't respect my work."

"It's not your work. And it's nothing personal, at least, it's not against you. It's me. I just don't happen to believe in romance."

"*Believe* in it?" For several seconds she stared at him incredulously, while he made no effort to defend his absurd statement. "What is there *not* to believe in? You don't believe men and women fall in love? That there's a certain magic in what they feel?"

At that moment, looking down into Charity's brown eyes, Lance would have liked to believe in romance, if for no other reason than that she believed in it, and that belief meant a great deal to her. But even for the sake of that spark of naive faith that glistened in her dark eyes, he couldn't pretend that reality could be founded in fantasy.

"I believe in sexual chemistry," he said. "Usually it's a sort of biological practical joke that brings men and women together with the most unlikely and inappropriate partners."

"People fall in love...."

"I concede that point. And they care about each other. Really care. It's the myth of happily ever after that I take issue with. Nothing lasts."

"Love does."

His face was set as if chiseled in stone, every feature hard and unyielding, and the scars that ordinarily enhanced his rugged handsomeness added to the impression of a frozen intractability that spread all the way to his mind. "Not even love, lady." His voice faded into a soft whisper that was intense with emotion as old memories invaded his mind. "Especially not love."

Charity heard the edge of remembered pain in his voice and fleetingly wondered what experience had hurt him so severely, fostered so much bitterness in him. But there was no place for pity in the middle of a confrontation. "It can," she answered, with equal conviction. "If two people work at it, love can last."

He dismissed her point with a shake of his head. "Obviously you haven't seen the divorce rate lately. Or the statistics on domestic violence."

"It doesn't last every time," she admitted, "but it can. Sometimes it does."

"In your books," he said, and, dropping his hand from her arm as though he'd forgotten he was touching her and realized he was making a mistake in doing so, he resumed walking.

Charity scurried to catch up with his longer strides. They'd aired half their differences. She'd be damned if he was just going to walk away without facing the other half. "I suppose you think the tragedy and stark reality in your work gives it some sort of special merit," she challenged. "Make people cry and you touch the truth?"

"It *was* nonfiction," he replied snidely.

"I'm not talking about truth in the sense of fiction or nonfiction. I mean in terms of the truth of human spirit and dignity and emotion. The universal truths that writers are supposed to touch."

He stopped again and positioned his scarred face above hers ominously, stopping her in her tracks. "Damn it, Charity, I don't want to fight with you. We're supposed to be writing a book, not looking for universal truths. Let's just write it."

The condescension in his voice as he quoted her raised an uncharacteristic ire in her. "Do you want to know why I was wary of this writing partnership?" she asked, itching to tell him.

"Not really."

Exasperation rushed from her lips in an extended sigh that was not quite a word, yet managed to convey her rage quite succinctly. "Yes, you do," she snapped. "You do, or you wouldn't have asked me if Tony had talked me into it."

"All right," he said. "I'll bite. What made you hesitate?"

"You," she said, and realized too late how revealing that answer was. Crossing her arms over her waist in a belligerent stance, she directed a vituperative scowl at him before attempting to talk her way out of the gaffe. "Between your condemnation of romance writing in your speech and your background as a cop, I couldn't see where we'd have much in common."

"What bothers you about my having been a cop?"

The tilt of his head as he looked at her indicated he was genuinely interested in her answer, and Charity felt her hard rage dissipating. "I'm not fond of violence or books that glamorize or aggrandize it. Since your first book was about cops, and it was rather raw, it was a natural assumption that your fiction would fall into the realm of blood and guts."

"Reality isn't your forte, is it?"

The question carried the flavor of an insult, and Charity's hackles rose accordingly. "I don't have any problems with reality."

Lance answered with a skeptical chuckle. "He sees her across a crowded room. She feels his eyes on her and turns." Crossing his hands over his heart in an exaggerated stage gesture, he gasped. "It's love at first sight!"

A pregnant silence followed his performance. Cautiously, Lance lowered his face to study Charity's, wondering if he'd gone too far. Their gazes locked, but her eyes gave him no clue as to what she was thinking. An apology was forming on his tongue when she spoke unexpectedly, in a gravelly voice.

"Spike shrank further back into the shadows and felt the hair on the back of his neck prickle as the footsteps got closer." Her eyes narrowed into slits, her hand came up, her forefinger extended to look like a gun. "His clammy hand closed even tighter around the gun. The weight of the weapon was reassuring. It was a big gun, powerful enough to blow a sizable hole in a man's chest. If, that is, Spike was quick enough. If his aim was steady. And if his finger wasn't too slippery with sweat to pull the trigger. Suddenly Dirk was in the alley, within range, his gun at the ready."

She pretended to aim and shoot. "Spike aimed, fired, felt the recoil of the gun. Dirk fell. Even in the dim light, Spike could make out the stain of blood spreading over the filthy concrete."

Her eyes met Lance's again across another significant silence. A lazy grin curled Lance's mouth and grew into a full-fledged smile. "Are you sure you don't want to do a blood and guts?"

Charity responded with a tinkle of laughter, and Lance laughed, too. "Truce?" he asked.

"Truce," she agreed.

Later Charity would reflect that it seemed much more than a truce, as though they'd agreed to call off the entire war. Lance cupped her elbow as they resumed their hike, guided her through the menu at the sandwich shop and insisted on buying both their meals. They chatted amiably on the walk back to his house.

She was comfortable with him after that, comfortable enough, in fact, that when they were discussing the story and he made the snide remark that a woman al-

ways meant trouble for a man, she propped her chin on
her hand and asked, "What soured you on love, Palmer?"

"I was in it once," he replied dryly.

"What happened?" she said without thinking, and
then, noting the way his mouth hardened as he searched
for the suitable answer, cursed the perverse curiosity
that had led her to ask such a probing personal question.

"We got married and didn't live happily ever after."
He frowned before continuing. "We didn't even live
miserably ever after. We just limped off in separate
directions rubbing our wounds." Another pause, a
deeper frown. "The rubbing didn't do any good; the
wounds still left scars."

Charity bit the inside of her lip to keep from asking
more questions, wondering why she was suddenly so
interested in the history of his love life. She told herself
it was because they were going to be working together
and she needed to understand what had molded his attitudes, but as much as she wanted to believe that ex-
planation, she couldn't. It wasn't Lance Palmer the
writing partner she was curious about, it was Lance
Palmer the man.

Why not? she thought, and instantly came up with
several good reasons. Tough guys weren't her type, for
one thing. She'd never been impressed by muscle and
brawn. They were business partners, for another. They
had a book to write, and anything beyond a business
relationship could jeopardize their work. And then
there were the legions of groupies that swooned around
him at conferences and autographings. A woman would
have to stand in line to sacrifice herself to his charm.

Still, she found herself studying him as he stared down at his hands, obviously still caught up in a labyrinth of bitter memories. His profile was craggy and strong, not quite handsome, but rugged and pristinely masculine.

Charity wanted to comfort him, to brush the lock of hair from his forehead and touch his cheek and say something trite but reassuring. She wanted to feel the roughness of the beard under her fingertips and, later, the swell of his lips against her own. Following his gaze to his steepled fingers, she remembered the gentleness of his strong hands during the odd moments he'd touched her, and wished she could feel those strong hands caressing her.

Her throat went dry as a gentle warmth swirled in ever widening circles from a source deep inside her. *He was right about sexual chemistry,* she thought, swallowing in an effort to moisten her mouth. *Sometimes it did seem like a biological practical joke, drawing you to the most inappropriate person.*

The renegade attraction to Lance annoyed her as she acknowledged it. Even if they should discover they had anything in common besides the book they were working on, Lance had given her no indication he was the brunt of the same practical joke her biological urges were playing on her.

She gathered the notes she had taken, tapping them on the table to straighten the edges before she put them in her portfolio. The shuffling drew Lance's attention and he turned to her. She stood up, straightening her spine into a posture that said their workday was officially over. "We've done enough brainstorming for today. Let's let the ideas perk a few days and then try to firm them up. Write down anything that seems promising, and I'll do the same. We'll compare notes next time, and maybe we can get the story line down pat.''

Lance pulled his feet from the railing and rose. He sounded relieved when he said, "Okay."

They decided on a time and date as he walked Charity to her car. There was a moment of awkwardness when they reached it. Lance sucked in a deep breath, exhaled heavily and said, "It was a productive session, wasn't it?"

Charity recognized it as a plea for reassurance rather than a statement made with conviction. She nodded and said, "We made a lot of headway."

Another awkward moment passed. It was not just the silence that contributed to the awkwardness, but a mutual self-consciousness. Charity squelched the absurd hope that Lance might be considering kissing her goodbye and noted wryly that the meeting had been too productive in some ways—some very personal ways. Lance finally cut through the awkwardness by reaching down to open the car door for her.

Charity gratefully settled into the driver's seat and devoted unnecessary attention to fastening the seat belt. She didn't roll down the window after he closed the door so they could talk, but, rather, waited until she had backed the car onto the road before waving goodbye to Lance. She watched him, a sturdy figure standing with legs apart and hands tucked into his back pockets, growing smaller in the rearview mirror, and was disproportionately pleased to note that he was watching her car disappear into the distance.

Chapter Four

By the time she returned to Lance's house the following Tuesday, Charity was satisfied that she had come up with some solid twists for the story they were plotting. She was also determined to no longer succumb to Lance Palmer's combination of guileless charm and blunt maleness. Chemistry with the right person might be magic, but a one-sided attraction to a man who preferred that a woman's bust measurement exceed her IQ and didn't believe in love was pure folly. If ignored, this crazy attraction she felt for Lance would shrivel from lack of encouragement, and she intended to ignore it and let it shrivel.

Sexual chemistry a perverse biological joke! If Lance Palmer truly believed that, it wasn't because he was a realist. It was because his bad experience with marriage had warped his attitude toward love and romance. If she erred in the direction of romance, he erred equally as far in the direction of cynicism. And if the subject came up again and turned into a verbal sparring match, she'd tell him as much.

There was no note on Lance's door this time, so she knocked. Immediately Tilly's excited barking filtered through the door, loud and menacing enough to intimidate prospective burglars. Charity heard Lance telling the dog to calm down just before the door opened in a powerful sweep and Lance stood before her, restraining Tilly by the collar. "See," he said to the dog. "It's Charity. You remember her." He gave Charity a slightly lopsided grin and said, "Every once in a while Tilly likes to pretend he's vicious."

"He's just doing his job," Charity said, putting out her hand. Recognizing her scent, the dog began wagging his tail in anticipation of being petted.

"Some protector," Lance said, with more affection than derision. "The coffee's brewed. Shall we pour and adjourn to the deck?"

They fell easily into the pattern set the week before, sitting in the patio chairs and sipping their coffee while they let the peaceful silence of the rural setting clear their minds before they began their work. At last, when the emptied mugs were placed side by side on the table, Lance said, "I've been thinking about the ideas we came up with last week. I like the diary bit. Lots of possibilities. It can be filled with information that could embarrass businessmen, politicians, you know, people with money and power."

"What's our heroine doing with it?"

"A hooker gave it to her."

"Why?"

"I haven't figured that out yet. Maybe she was being chased and gave it to the heroine in a ladies' room somewhere."

"I like the idea of a hooker giving her a diary," Charity said. "There's a Pandora's box of possibilities there. But I don't think it should be random. How would the bad guys know the hooker no longer had the diary? And how would they trace it to the heroine? And if she's just randomly involved, wouldn't she just give it to the first person who threatened to beat her up? She certainly wouldn't go running after it if it were stolen."

"Maybe the call girl's a relative, a sister. Or maybe the diary has information in it about the heroine's brother or some lousy boyfriend she's trying to protect."

Charity said, "Logic, Palmer. Think. The call girl would have to have a reason to give up the diary in the first place. Whom would she give it to, and why?"

After a long, thoughtful pause, Lance said, "She'd give it to someone for safekeeping if she couldn't keep it safe herself for some reason, especially if she was keeping it as sort of a retirement fund. If she was going into the hospital . . ."

"Or arrested," Charity said, enthused. "If she had been arrested unexpectedly, she'd ask her attorney to hold it."

"God," Lance said. "A lawyer? We can't write about a cop, but we can write about a lawyer?"

"It makes sense," Charity said. "This society madame is arrested and sends her attorney to get the diary out of her safe before the cops can get a search warrant and find it while they're looking for something else."

"What?"

"Whatever they're looking for. Hot jewelry. Fake currency."

"Maybe the feds are after her for unreported income," Lance offered.

"Would the feds arrest her before they had a search warrant?"

"Who knows what the feds'll do?"

Charity shrugged. "We'll work out why she was arrested later. The basic scenario works. We have the heroine going in and getting the diary before the cops find it, and someone snatching it from the heroine. Now how do we get the hero involved?"

"Maybe he's in the diary."

"That's not very heroic," Charity said. "Why don't we just let him stumble into the whole setup?"

"You mean, he sees someone strong-arming the girl and leaps to her rescue."

"Something like that."

"It's certainly typical," Lance said rather grumpily.

"Typical as in cliché?" Charity asked.

"No. I mean, the best intentions in the world tend to turn into chaos when a woman's involved."

"I'm going to forget you said that," she said, and Lance merely harrumphed. A protracted silence followed, then Charity, briskly businesslike, said, "He's going to need some motivation to remain involved in the situation. Otherwise she'd just thank him for his intentions and he'd be on his merry way after the bad guys get away with the diary."

"She's a good-looking woman...."

"Oh, yes. A broad-chested redhead. But no guy's going to get involved in something like this over a little cleavage."

Lance shook his head skeptically. "We're talking a *lot* of cleavage."

"Get serious, would you?"

Lance laughed aloud. "Touchy on that subject, aren't you?"

"I'm touchy on the subject of getting this book plotted."

"Yes, ma'am," he said, with exaggerated deference and a tincture of indignation. He'd only been trying to have a little fun while they worked. Jeez, but she was hard to read. She was so cute today, wearing jeans again and an oversize T-shirt with panda bears on it that sort of clung to the right places and proved she had no reason to be prickly about some fictional woman's chest. He'd thought she looked ready for a little fun. Obviously, he'd been wrong.

"You're a man," she said.

"Nice of you to notice."

"Think. What would get a man involved in a madcap chase?"

"Besides a woman? Either money or a car."

"A car," Charity mused. "I like that. Men are so involved with their cars, like they're an extension of themselves."

"Now who's being chauvinistic?"

"It's a fact," Charity said. "Some men..."

"And some women," Lance insisted. "You're talking to an ex-cop here. I worked enough traffic to know women are as nuts about their cars as men."

"Touché. I still like the car as a device to get him involved. But how?"

They thought a moment. Lance shifted in his chair. "Suppose these thugs approach her on the sidewalk and grab her briefcase and she does the most likely thing and screams bloody murder..." Charity exhaled an exasperated sigh, but Lance continued undaunted. "And our hero, who happens to have just parked his car at the curb, runs over to help her, and the thugs try to get away but their car has a flat."

"That's a bit convenient," Charity observed.

"Well, for some reason, they knock the guy down and make him give them his keys and drive off in his car, so he's hopping mad as hell, so he and the heroine jump in some other guy's car and chase them."

"They lose them, of course," Charity added, "but then they drive around until they spy his car and steal up to the house and then—" She sighed again, as if worn out. "What happens then?"

"They ring the doorbell."

"Brilliant. But no one answers."

"Of course not," Lance agreed. "So then they look in the windows and..."

"Someone conks them on the head?"

"Which really ticks our hero off when he wakes up with a headache."

"People get conked on the head all the time in movies and on TV—is that really feasible?"

"There are ways," Lance said. "Military vets might know how, or accomplished karate buffs or cops."

"Or ex-cops."

Lance shrugged. "Actually, it's pretty iffy. If you slip up, you could kill someone, or else knock them out too lightly and they'll be back up and at your throat in a second."

"The conking bothers me."

"I think you said something to that effect the last time head-conking entered the conversation."

"That was Neanderthal conking, something very different. Still, if there was another way..."

"There's always chloroform or sodium Pentothal."

"Right! Of course. We're not dealing with hard-core criminals, just with people who have a vested interest in the diary. A prominent doctor—or, better yet, a psychiatrist—would have access to drugs and musclemen who might be persuaded to snitch a diary. He wouldn't want to hurt anybody or go to jail as an accomplice for grand auto theft or possible murder. He just wants the diary. So if they wake up somewhere far removed from his house, and the hero's car is wiped clean of fingerprints, they have no evidence to prove he was involved in anything."

"They wake up in his car on some deserted road in the middle of nowhere?"

"No," Charity decided. "They would take them back to where they found them."

"Too dangerous," said Lance. "Someone might see the two asleep and become suspicious."

"Not," said Charity, pointing a finger into the air, "if they were in the trunk of the car."

"Oh, come on."

"It's logical. The hero and heroine are out cold, and the thugs put them in the trunk knowing that by the time the two wake up and get out, the thugs will be long gone."

Lance's brow was furrowed with concentration. "It would work," Charity said. "Unless they'd smother. Trunks aren't airtight, are they?"

"No. The big danger would be heat, but if they were parked in the shade they'd be okay for a few hours. But a lot of trendy cars don't have trunks big enough to hold two people."

"Not comfortably. But these two are out cold, remember?"

"Most bodies that go into trunks are dead first."

"But not every time," Charity persisted.

"No. We had a hostage case once, where they left the woman in the trunk of a car."

"Then it's feasible."

"Yes. Provided we find a car with an adequate trunk."

"What are the hot cars these days? Rule out the sports cars."

"BMWs."

"Too pat," Charity said.

"Mercedes?"

"Maybe. How about something a little less...a little flashier."

"Camaros are hot now, but they don't have trunks. Pontiac makes some pretty flashy cars. Trans Am, Firebird."

"What kind of trunks do they have?"

"I've got a friend who sells them. We could check it out."

"Great!"

Lance was already out of his chair and walking to the house. "I'll give him a call."

"There's no hurry."

Undaunted, Lance said, "If he's off today, maybe he'll drive over. If he's not home I'll just leave a message on his answering machine."

He returned a few minutes later. "He was home. He's going to think about it and bring out a car this afternoon. All I had to do was suggest he bring his fishing rod with him, and Eddie was halfway out the door."

"Sounds as though you and he go back a long way."

"We were at the academy together." *And propped each other up through weddings and divorces together later on,* he thought.

"He was a cop, too?"

"Yeah. We were partners for a long time." A frown hardened Lance's mouth momentarily and then disappeared. "He left the force before I did." Settling into his chair, he hoisted his feet onto the railing and said, "Where do we go from here with the story?"

"Now that our heroine has an occupation, we could pick a name for her. What do you think—something very proper and lawyerish, or just the opposite?"

"I vote for something kind of...I don't know... unusual. Fritzi. Or Shea."

"I love it! Shea. For her mother's maiden name, of course. Very *haute rigeur*. Mixed with something a bit imposing. Van something or other."

"Christopherson?"

"Shea Christopherson," Charity tried aloud. "It doesn't scan well. We need something with one or two syllables. Shea Lake... Shea Smythefield... Shea..."

"Malone."

Charity giggled. "Shea Malone sounds like she might have been a moll for one of Al Capone's gang."

"Let's just keep Shea and think about the last name then. What about our hero?"

"Oh, you mean the svelte, dark-haired hunk?" Charity asked, grinning mischievously.

"We could name him Dudley Do-right or Noble Earnest," Lance suggested.

"We don't have a profession for him yet. I think he should wear a suit to work. Accountant?"

"How about a banker?"

"Okay. A banker. So what's his name?"

"Something solid, not wimpish. How about Tom or Robert or Sam?"

"Robert Something-respectable."

"Robert Erskine."

"Telephone call for you, Mr. Erskine," Charity said with a secretarial air. "Very impressive. I like it."

"Tremaine," Lance said.

"I beg your pardon?"

"For our heroine. Shea Tremaine. Has a colonial sound to it."

Charity was shuffling through the papers spread over the table. "Let's get all this down." When she'd finished with the character-information forms, she took out her notes. "Are you ready to try to rough out a loose plot?"

Working with Lance Palmer, Charity discovered, was vastly different from sitting alone and wracking her brain to background music by Tchaikovsky and Rachmaninoff, neither of whom had ever offered her an opinion, provided her with a unique perspective, enlightened her with a stroke of pure creative genius or argued with her over a plot twist. Even O.J., for all his rubbing against her legs while she sat at her desk or curling up in the crook of her knees as she sat on the sofa, had never cracked a joke or laughed with her when something that seemed logical at first glance turned out to be absurd upon closer examination.

The compromise inherent in meshing two perspectives and thought trains into a single story demanded the discipline of objectivity and sacrifice, yet Charity never felt Lance was forcing her to do more than a fair share of yielding in the process of give and take. Charity had not expected such fairness from him, and as his fair-mindedness revealed itself, she felt the apprehension she'd brought into the partnership gradually evolving into trust.

Hours passed as they roughed out the story line for the book. Charity leaned back in her chair, sighed and said, "With just a little more fleshing out, we'll be ready to start writing the synopsis."

Lance, who had stood up and now was stretching with the lethargy of a bear emerging from a cave after hibernation, said, "Not bad for a morning's work."

Charity rose and unconsciously raised her hand to rub the tense muscles in her neck. "I can't believe we've been sitting here over three hours."

"Turn around," Lance said. "I'll work that kink out for you."

His large fingers were surprisingly gentle as he kneaded her neck. At first Charity was aware only of a soothing sensation as her knotted muscles relaxed under his ministrations, and she sighed gratefully. "Where did you learn that?"

"One-hour demonstration in physical-stress management at the academy."

"Long live the academy!" Charity said, not realizing that she was instinctively moving closer to the source of those comforting sensations. She became aware first of the masculine warmth of Lance's body behind her, and then that the sensations his touch was stirring in her no longer were simple comfort. And then, abruptly, the kneading motion of Lance's fingers stopped.

He's trying to decide whether to kiss me, Charity thought with absolute certainty, and she herself struggled with the choice between turning around and tilting her face toward his, encouraging him, or remaining still, giving Lance total responsibility for the decision.

She didn't turn around, but it was a struggle, and the seconds she waited to see what Lance would do seemed interminable. He drew his hand away from her neck and she heard his indrawn breath of resolve before he said, "I got some ground round. I thought we'd grill hamburgers for lunch."

Charity, too, sucked in a silent breath before answering. "Sounds delicious." Later, while foraging through the produce drawer for a tomato to slice, she said, "You cleaned your refrigerator."

"I read up on salmonella," Lance said dryly on his way to the deck with the meat patties. "It has nothing to do with salmon!" he called back from outside.

Charity laughed, but the laughter faded quickly as she worked in the privacy of the small kitchen and pondered the phenomenon of how much she enjoyed Lance's company. Was it wise? Was it dangerous? Did it matter?

She liked Lance, she enjoyed being with him, she was disappointed that he hadn't kissed her. These were facts—and facts, like taxes, celebrity and sexual chemistry, were not subject to the whim of reason or analysis. Facts simply must be accepted as facts, so Charity accepted the fact that she liked Lance and was sexually attracted to him.

And she wondered why he hadn't kissed her.

Eddie Greenwood arrived just as they were finishing their meal. Lance answered the door and after the usual rush of masculine banter, the two of them entered the kitchen. "Eddie, this is Charity Lovejoy. She and I are working on a book together."

Eddie, who had a thick thatch of auburn hair, a boyish face, freckled skin and a nice smile, looked at Charity but spoke to Lance as he shook Charity's hand. "You son of a gun. You've been holding out. When you left the force and talked about this writing thing, you never mentioned beautiful coauthors."

"It's a new development," Lance said. "We have the same agent, and he thought Charity could teach me a few tricks about fiction. She's a college professor as well as an author. You can let go of her now, Eddie."

Eddie acted as though he hadn't realized he was still holding Charity's right hand and told her, "Sorry. Guess I just got lost in those big eyes of yours."

"You're timing's lousy, as usual," Lance said, clearly used to Eddie's flamboyance. "We just finished lunch, but I can stir up enough heat on the coals for one more patty if you're hungry."

"I'm always hungry," Eddie said. He settled into the chair opposite Charity's and was staring at her transfixed.

"Give the lady a break, Eddie. She's not used to you yet," Lance said, as he formed a hunk of meat into a patty. "Just humor him, Charity. We're hoping to have him fit for human society by the turn of the century." On the way to the deck, he casually dropped the words, "She writes romance novels."

"No fooling?" Eddie asked. "You mean the sexy kind?"

Lance paused at the door. "They call her the emerging grand mistress of the sensuous, sensitive sex scene." Charity shot him an exasperated glare, and he countered with a mischievous smile.

Eddie, still staring, propped his elbow on the table and his chin on his hand and said, "You're not married or anything, are you?"

Charity found his benign outrageousness amusing. "Not even anything."

"Anytime you need help researching those hot love scenes—"

"Has anyone ever volunteered to help you with research before?" Lance said, joining them at the table.

Charity grinned at him. "Once or twice." Then, to Eddie, she said sweetly, "I'll put your name on the waiting list."

"And I'll make sure she has your phone number if she needs it," Lance said. "Now why don't you give the lady a break and mind your manners. She's not one of the women from the Fast Cat."

"Jeez," Eddie said. "I haven't thought about the Fast Cat in years. How many years ago was that?"

"A couple of centuries," Lance said. "The Fast Cat," he explained to Charity, "was over on Nebraska Avenue, in our first patrol area when we were rookies."

"Talk about a hole!" Eddie said. "This place was pure sleaze. We only went in it when we didn't have any choice. Remember how Katy and Wanda used to fume every time we mentioned the place?"

The mood of jovial nostalgia disintegrated as Lance said bitterly, "Yeah. I remember."

Eddie's high spirits also wilted like a punctured balloon, and he sighed morosely. "Maybe we mentioned it once too often, huh?"

"Yeah," Lance said. "Maybe we did."

After an almost unbearable silence, Eddie shifted in his seat and said, "Hey, that was a long time ago. Tell me about this new book you're working on. What do you and the lady here need a hot car with a generous trunk for?"

"We want to see if a couple of bodies would fit inside."

"No fooling?" Eddie asked, and then, urgently, "Is that my hamburger that's on fire?"

Uttering an oath, Lance sprang up and dashed to the deck to check on the meat. "How bad is it?" Eddie called.

"You like your meat crispy, don't you?"

Eddie used the same oath Lance had, but Lance reentered the house, smiling. "Caught it just in time to turn it over. Why don't you get your bun ready?"

Eddie cocked his eyebrows lecherously at Charity. "What do you say, baby? Want to butter my buns for me, spread on a little mustard?"

"The lady's not your mother or the cook," Lance said, walking toward the kitchen. "I'll fix the roll if you're too lazy to do it yourself."

The familiarity of long-term friendship was apparent in Lance's attitude, but there was something else in the statement, too, a hint of possessiveness, a subtle, male-to-male type of communication that said, "Watch yourself, you're trespassing in my territory."

Charity propped her chin on her fist and contemplated what the possessiveness meant, and decided it was probably a sign that Lance thought of her as a partner, and of partners as inviolable and sacrosanct.

Eventually the men finished in the kitchen, and Lance went back to tend the grill. Eddie sat down at the table. "Tell me about this book you're writing. You know, some people would think it's a little strange when someone calls up and asks what model car has a trunk big enough to hold two bodies."

Charity summarized the scenario for him briefly.

"I looked at three different models and decided on the Grand Am," Eddie said. "You two can look it over."

They waited for Eddie to eat his burger, then trouped outside to examine the Grand Am. Eddie opened the trunk and removed his fishing gear, then the three of them stood peering into the trunk as though they expected some spirit to materialize and rise up from where the spare tire was kept.

"What do you think?" Charity asked.

"It's a close call," Lance said.

Eddie offered his opinion. "No problem if they were unconscious. You'd never get them in there kicking and screaming."

"Charity?" Lance prompted.

"I don't know. Probably, but..."

"Why don't you climb in and try it out?" Eddie cracked.

Lance looked at Charity. Charity looked at Lance. Lance lifted his eyebrows and his shoulders. Charity lifted her eyebrows and her shoulders.

"We could," Lance said, fixing his eyes on Charity's face. "Charity?"

Charity recognized a dare when she heard it. Lance no more believed she would climb into that trunk with him than he believed she would sprout wings and fly.

But Lance didn't know Charity as well as he thought.

"It might strengthen the scene," she said. "If we actually experienced being in the trunk, we'd be able to describe it more accurately, with more sensuous detail."

The expression on Lance's face was priceless. Charity enjoyed it immensely as she watched him struggle for something to say. *Who's daring whom, Mr. Palmer?* she thought smugly.

Eddie draped an arm across Charity's shoulders. "If you want a stand-in, old buddy, you can work the key and Charity and I..."

Lance grinned. "Sorry, Eddie. Some things a man just has to do for himself. I agree with Charity. If we actually get in we'll be able to describe it more accurately. I'll get in the trunk with Charity and you can close the lid once we're in and let us out when we knock."

"You trust this turkey, don't you?" Charity whispered, while Eddie was carrying his fishing gear to the deck. "I wouldn't want to get locked in for real."

"I've trusted him with my life a number of times."

Eddie returned and the three of them stared into the trunk again. *I can't believe this is happening,* Charity thought.

"Any preference as to top or bottom?" Lance asked.

Charity turned to Eddie. "If you had two unconscious people, which one would you put in the trunk first?"

"The heaviest," he said.

Charity looked at Lance. "After you, Hemingway."

Scrunching his long body into the short width of the trunk, Lance said, "Remember that our hero is shorter and slimmer than I am."

"Our heroine is taller and, er, *broader* than I am, so it evens out," Charity said, eyeing the opening of the trunk warily as she pondered the most expedient way to climb inside. Insanity. That's what this was. Sheer insanity.

"Comfy?" Eddie asked Lance, with irritating amusement.

"As comfortable as I'm going to get," Lance replied, and then mumbled something not quite unintelligible that ended with, "damned sardine."

Charity was resigned to the fact that she was going to have to crawl into the trunk. The critical question now was, how? Acknowledging with a sinking feeling that there was no graceful way to do it, she swallowed to get rid of the lump in her throat and put one foot on the fender, ready to hitch herself up and over the rim of the trunk.

"Permit me," Eddie said, gallantly giving her a boost by cupping his hand under her elbow to steady her as she climbed into the trunk.

Clenching her jaw, she arranged herself into the limited space above Lance, hoping she wasn't inadvertently poking any inconvenient areas of his anatomy with her elbows or knees.

Eddie was standing at the tail of the car peering down at them, his hand resting lightly on the lid to the trunk. "It's going to be a close fit," he observed. Then, lightly, he asked Lance, "You okay down there? Not dying of ecstasy or anything?"

"No complaints," Lance said exasperatedly. "Just close the damned lid."

"Tough job, writing," Eddie said as he guided the lid down. Just over halfway, he bent over and poked his face near the remaining slit of an opening and said, "You okay, Charity? The hinges aren't pressing into your back?"

"I'm okay," she said, and a second later the lid clicked shut and she was alone with Lance, pressed against him in pitch blackness.

Gravity, the natural force that pulls all things toward the earth, took on a new meaning in Charity's mind. While the floor of the trunk effectively stopped Lance's fall to the earth, Lance's body was what stopped Charity's. Gravity was pulling at her, and the lid of the trunk was pushing on her back, and yet she was aware that her body touched Lance's in a way that had nothing to do with gravity or the book they were writing. Thank God it was dark so he couldn't see her face—couldn't see the raw sexual response to him that her eyes would undoubtedly betray. There were plenty of air pockets in the trunk, but breathing was difficult for reasons that had nothing to do with the oxygen supply.

The warmth of his body under hers, the solidity of it, the scent of him were omnipotent. His physical presence permeated her senses. She wondered fleetingly if Lance was as affected by the forced proximity, but she was not left guessing for long. Women can keep some secrets more easily than men, especially in the dark.

The irrefutable evidence of his response to her overwhelmed her, and made her even more aware of him. "Lance?" she whispered.

"Yes," he confirmed succinctly.

Charity's heart beat wildly, blood pulsed through her body, heat rose in her face. She knew she must say something, but wondered how she would possibly force words through such an impossibly dry throat. *Humor,* she told herself. *Try humor.*

"That . . ." She had to swallow to moisten her throat and begin again. "That's not a flashlight between us, is it?"

Lance was not amused. His voice was unusually husky as he said, irritably, "No."

Charity swallowed again. "I was afraid of that."

The silence that followed was excruciatingly awkward. Charity wrote about mindless, magic desire, but she'd never be able to put what she was feeling at the moment into words. Letters on paper would never capture such an overwhelming awareness that he was a man and she was a woman. It was that fundamentally simple, and that fundamentally complex. She was, after all, supposed to be his writing partner, not his paramour.

And he had deliberately decided *not* to kiss her that very day.

His writing partner. In her panic she sought refuge in their work and said, "This might be a good place for the first k—" But the last word was smothered by Lance's mouth as it instinctively found hers in the absolute darkness, and the devastating effect of his kiss usurped her senses and her mind.

It was not a kiss that began gently and escalated in its intensity. It was, from the first instant their lips met, demanding, stirring and thorough. Charity's mobility was limited in the small area, but she managed to cradle his face in her hands, savoring the feel of his flesh under her fingertips. Lance somehow maneuvered one arm around her and the opposite hand behind her head where he threaded his fingers through her hair. His lips left hers only long enough for him to whisper her name before finding her mouth again and resuming the hungry assault on her senses.

Charity felt as though nothing existed beyond the two of them pressed together in the small space, beyond the firmness of Lance's body next to hers and the urgency of their need for each other. She had written about sexual magic, long, descriptive, flowery passages about passion and ardor, yet she'd never been so thoroughly cloaked in the mesmerizing spell of that magic. It was not technique that was assailing her senses and leaving her vulnerable to this languor, but Lance himself; she was reacting to the very essence of his personality, to the intangibles that made him an individual instead of merely a male presence.

His lips left hers, and he groaned. Charity let her forehead drop against his breastbone and sighed as though exhausted from a long battle, then rested her cheek on his chest and listened to the rhythm of his strong heartbeat beneath her ear. His fingers were still tangled in her hair and he idly massaged her scalp.

She said his name, but he made a shushing sound and kissed the top of her head and made the sound again, more emphatically. "Don't say a word," came the whispered entreaty, and he repeated it even more softly.

Charity understood his need for absolute silence in the absolute darkness. The magic still lingered, swaddled around them like a cocoon of contentment, and words would only shatter the spell. She sighed again and snuggled her cheek into his chest, perfectly willing to bask in the magic with him a bit longer.

Eddie's slap on the top of the trunk lid reverberated like the stroke of a Chinese gong and Charity jerked in surprise and bashed her head in the process. She was hardly finished saying, "Ouch!" when the key turned in the lock and the lid sprang open, letting in a blinding avalanche of sunshine.

Grinning from ear to ear, Eddie said jovially, "Well, did you have fun, boys and girls?" Charity wanted to slug him, and noted out of the corner of her eye that Lance looked as though he might.

With Eddie's assistance, she climbed out, and then Lance unfolded like a corpse rising from a coffin and climbed out, stretching kinks from his muscles. Rubbing his right buttock with the flat of his hand, he said,

"When we write the scene, remind me to mention the bolt that holds the cover over the spare tire. I think it left a permanent impression."

"Is that what you were moaning and groaning about?" Charity asked wryly, and enjoyed the look of astonishment that crossed Lance's face.

Chapter Five

You guys ready to raid the beer and bait and hit the gulf, or do you need to make extensive notes on your experiment first?" Eddie asked.

Lance, still agog at Charity's offhand humor, looked at Eddie as though he'd spoken in a foreign language.

"You did say we were going fishing, didn't you?" Eddie said.

"Oh, sure. We're going," said Lance. He turned to Charity. "Did you want to work a while longer?"

Charity knew where work and fishing fell on the ladder of male priorities. "Eddie drove all the way from Tampa with the carrot of fishing dangling in front of his nose. I think you'd better take him fishing," she said.

Eddie appeared genuinely surprised as he asked, "You're not coming with us?"

That perplexed look claimed Lance's face again, but he recovered and said, "Of course, you're welcome to

come along. I've got an extra rod, and we can get you a
license at the general store when we stop for—''

''Beer and bait,'' Charity finished for him, amused.
''Sorry, guys. At the risk of sounding sexist, beer and
bait has a distinctively male ring to it, and I have some
shopping to do, so I think I'll hit the mall to strike my
blow for equal rights. Thanks anyway. I'll just get my
things from the house.''

The moment she reached the haven of the house,
Charity sagged against the door, took a deep, fortifying breath and offered a silent prayer of thanks for a
moment of solitude. Delayed reaction was setting in.

What a man!

What a kiss!

What a god-awful mess! The romantic and the cynic.
Lord, where did they go from here?

She peeled herself away from the door and squared
her shoulders before crossing the room for her purse
and portfolio. Lance was going fishing, and she was
going to the mall—that's where! And, with any luck,
after she'd spent a few hours shopping and possibly
dining out with a friend, sanity would miraculously be
restored to her and she would put the kiss into perspective. It might seem like an earth-moving, senses-
shattering celestial experience now, but later, when she
was capable of rational thought, she'd see it for what it
was: earth-moving, senses-shattering folly.

The men were in the garage sorting through Lance's
tackle box when she went outside, and she waved as she
walked to her car. Eddie waved back and called, ''Nice
meeting you.'' Lance dropped the hook he was fid-
dling with and ran to catch up with her.

''I hope you don't mind cutting the day short.''

''We put in a respectable day's work this morning.''

They reached the car. Lance shoved his hands in his hip pockets and Charity felt his hesitation before he spoke. "About what happened—"

"Were you as surprised as I was?" she asked lightly.

Lance's eyes slid knowingly over her face. "Were you surprised?"

Charity ignored the question and got in the car. After starting the engine, she rolled down the window. "Just for the record," she said, "I already have a fishing license."

This time, she did not watch the reflected image of Lance shrink in the rearview mirror as she pressed the accelerator. She was wracked suddenly by a tremor of relief, the kind of relief that comes on the heels of a narrow escape. She switched on the radio and turned up the volume until the music reverberated through the car and her mind, leaving no room for thoughts of Lance Palmer and the hardness of his body against hers, of the strength of his hands as they touched her and the taste of his lips on hers.

Blaring rock music, though, proved only a temporary respite from the disturbingly sensuous memories, and at length she turned down the radio to avoid damaging her hearing. No use trying to forget the unforgettable. Damn, seven months ago she'd stood in Miami watching women flock around Lance and wondered what they saw in such a brawny, opinionated giant. Groupies, awed by the combination of bulging biceps and a Pulitzer prize nomination. Miffed by his cheap shots at the work she did, she'd felt immune to the enigmatic contrasts that made Lance so alluring. And now—

She sighed deeply. So their foray into "experience-it" research had lead to a little hands-on role-playing. So what? It was probably nothing to Lance. Hell, he'd probably done what he figured a macho guy would be expected to do when he was squashed into indecent intimacy in a car trunk with a woman.

The line of that old song about a kiss being just a kiss skittered absurdly through her mind. Ha! Not some kisses, and not to some people. Certainly not that soul-searing kiss in the car trunk, and not to Charity Lovejoy, the emerging grand mistress of the sensuous, sizzling sex scene. But to Lance Palmer—

She frowned mightily. To Lance Palmer, a little lip-to-lip massage was probably just a little lip-to-lip massage. Nothing personal. Certainly nothing serious. Situation normal, female all fluffed up over a little fooling around in the trunk of a car. Normal for Lance Palmer, who had females fawning over him, batting their eyes at him, asking for his autograph and doubtless offering more than a casual sigh in return.

Mile after mile Charity scowled at the highway ahead of her, disgusted with herself for remaining so preoccupied over an experience Lance had probably already forgotten or, worse, was regretting. Hadn't he brought it up almost apologetically when he'd walked her to the car, as though he were regretting it? At least she'd handled it well, affecting an air of casualness and managing the attitude of "So what?" that the situation had cried for.

After a few miles of thickening traffic, the mall came into view, and Charity sighed with relief. Department stores. Card shops. Soda fountains. Cozy little boutiques. Bookstores. Deliverance. No wonder these shrines to commerce and capitalism were referred to as the psychiatrist's couch of the eighties!

Charity found an empty parking slot three spaces from the main entrance and took it as an omen of good fortune. And indeed, she was lucky enough to find exactly what she was shopping for at a bargain price.

Sylvia Rook, a full-time faculty member at the junior college where Charity taught creative writing, was getting a divorce, and her ex-husband had gotten custody of their king-size bed. Sylvia had bought a twin bed as a symbol of her new solitary life-style, and Charity found the perfect gift of twin-size percale sheets splashed with bold geometric shapes. After paying for them, she took them to have them wrapped and, while the present was being wrapped, telephoned to invite Sylvia to meet her for dinner.

Later, they met and found a cozy spot for their meal. "What a wonderful idea," Sylvia said. "Dinner out on a Tuesday night. It's sinfully indulgent. Mike and I never..." Pausing at the mention of her ex-husband, she shrugged away the reference to him and began the sentence anew. "I'm not used to going out on weeknights." And then, resolutely, she added, "Maybe it'll become a habit."

Charity raised her glass. "To new habits."

"To new habits," Sylvia said, lifting her glass to touch Charity's. And then, when they'd drunk the toast and put their glasses back on the table, Sylvia said, "So tell me about your latest book."

"It's a collaboration," Charity said. "Lance Palmer and I are working on a romantic, suspenseful romp."

"Lance Palmer? *The Cost of Being a Cop* Lance Palmer?"

"One and the same," Charity said. "Did you read it?"

"Read it—I absorbed it," Sylvia said. "I even braved one of those dreary library luncheons to hear him speak. Believe me, it was anything but dreary once he got up to talk. He had the audience eating out of his hand."

"A predominantly female audience, no doubt," Charity said.

"Oh, yes. He's very charming. And very sexy. What's he like to work with?"

"I've always worked solo, so having a partner takes some getting used to," Charity said evasively.

Before Sylvia could push for any specific details, the waiter brought them their food, and Charity mused that if she could have afforded it, she would tip him double for his timing. She managed to guide the conversation away from Lance as they ate, and then, as they were luxuriating over after-dinner coffee, she said, "It's early yet. Let's go to my house and have an old-fashioned gab session."

"You talked me into it," Sylvia said. "My first class isn't until ten tomorrow morning anyway."

Soon after their arrival at Charity's place, Charity thrust a gaily wrapped package toward her friend. "What's this?" Sylvia asked.

"It's a...I was about to say it's a divorce present, but that's not the right word," Charity answered, looking up from pouring wine into stemmed glasses. "It's an *independence* present."

"Sheets!" Sylvia said, dumbfounded. "Twin-size sheets! Oh, Charity, only you would think of something so...apropos." Tears welled in her eyes. "You knew exactly what I needed. It's so difficult, you know, declaring independence after fifteen years...."

"But what the hell," Charity said expansively, giving Sylvia one of the glasses, "adversity strengthens the character. Let's toast adversity! And a new, stronger you."

"I'll drink to that," Sylvia said and, catching Charity's reckless mood, giggled. "And now I want to hear every detail about your work with Lance Palmer."

"Nothing's more boring than a writer talking about writing."

Sylvia giggled again. "I don't want you to talk about writing. I want you to talk about Lance Palmer. Did you think I wouldn't notice how you changed the subject back at the restaurant? Come on. I may be divorced, but I'm not tuned into being single again yet, so help me live vicariously. Tell me all about working with that delicious hunk."

"How much wine have you had?" Charity said, laughter in her voice.

"Not enough to miss how you changed the subject earlier. Let's have some juicy details—is something brewing here?"

While Charity and Sylvia were sipping wine and giggling like schoolgirls over Charity's provocative report on the episode in the car trunk, Lance and Eddie were nursing the last of a six-pack after eating fresh flounder for dinner. Eddie had drunk just enough beer to wax nostalgic. "You miss the force?" he asked Lance.

After a pause, Lance said, "Sometimes. Not too much. How about you?"

Eddie took a long swig of beer. "Yeah. I miss it. Sometimes I wonder if I should send out a few letters and see if some department would take me. Some metro forces are begging for experienced officers. Even if I had to start out with rookie status . . . well, selling cars is okay, but inside, I'm a cop. It's all I ever wanted to be.''

"Have you considered reapplying at Tampa? Political climates change; you might go right back on duty with your former grade.''

Eddie was one of the cops Lance had written about, the one he'd called Joe in his book. He'd been caught in a political squeeze over a questionable shooting and more or less asked to resign voluntarily to save the department embarrassment—and certain politicians some bad press.

Actually, there had been nothing questionable about the shooting in Eddie's mind or the minds of any of the other officers on the force. Eddie had violated no departmental policy by shooting at a fleeing felon. In fact, considering that the felon was known to be armed and had initiated fire before turning to flee, there was no reason the shooting would have drawn more than the routine review, except that the felon had been black and the shooting had occurred in an election year in a part of town where racial tension was high.

Unfortunately there were officers on the force who were racially prejudiced and probably deserved censure, but Lance knew Eddie wasn't one of them. Eddie had just been a cop doing his job. But he'd had the misfortune to become a scapegoat, which made the whole incident even sadder.

"I couldn't go back to Tampa," Eddie said, drawing Lance back into the present. "Even if they'd reinstate me, I couldn't go back." Grinning lopsidedly, he teased, "Besides, my old partner wouldn't be there. If I've got to change partners, I might as well change entire departments. Who knows—maybe I'll get as lucky with partners as you did.''

It took Lance a moment to grasp his meaning. "Charity?"

"What a looker," Eddie said. "Say, I'm sorry I brought up Katy in front of her. I wasn't thinking about what I was saying. You two making it or what?"

Usually Eddie's bluntness bounced off Lance like basketballs from a backboard, but Lance found this particular question an unforgivable intrusion on his privacy. Feeling the hairs prickle on the back of his neck, he tried to sound casual. "Not yet, but I'm working on it."

Since when, old buddy? he asked himself, but he knew the answer: *Since you walked into Tony's hotel room and saw her sitting there all prim and proper and utterly untouchable, that's when.*

"Working kind of slow, aren't you?"

"Some things can't be rushed," Lance said brusquely. "Charity Lovejoy is one of them."

"You're a mite touchy on the subject," Eddie said, his voice a trifle smug. "She getting under your skin?"

"She's not under my skin," Lance said, but now that he thought about it, he felt her wedged there, a nagging presence that couldn't be ignored.

Eddie drained his beer, crushed the can and tossed it. It dropped dead center into the trash can and hit the plastic bottom with a dull thud. "Two points," he said, then added slyly, "the last time you were this coy about a woman was right after you met Katy."

Lance jerked to attention. "There's no comparison, Eddie. You're way off."

"Whatever you say," Eddie said, "but it sounds to me like I stepped on the truth or something. Any more beer in the fridge?"

"Sorry," Lance said, "that was the last one."

"Just as well," Eddie said with a shrug. "I've got a long drive ahead of me in a little while."

"I'll put a pot of coffee on to brew," Lance offered, suddenly impatient for Eddie to leave.

"I got a Christmas card from Wanda and that wimp she married. No note or anything, just a formal signature. 'Mr. and Mrs. Jacob Irelander.' You ever hear from Katy and God's gift to the Indiana justice system?"

"Yeah, I hear from her," Lance said, the words bloated with bitterness. "She even writes notes."

"Under the circumstances, I guess she'd have to."

"No. She doesn't *have* to. That's the hell of it, knowing that she doesn't *have* to do it. But, hell, Katy was always fair, and I guess when a woman's married to a judge—"

"Yeah," said Eddie. "I guess so."

Chapter Six

Charity was trying to watch a talk show, but couldn't get interested in the burning issue of the day. She changed the channel, only to discover that she was even less interested in the next one she began to watch. Further clicks of the tuner brought her a manic game show, home shopping and reruns of an old situation comedy. She turned off the set and plumped the decorator pillows on the sofa.

Habit led her to her office, a blatantly feminine room with an old-fashioned secretarial desk huge enough to accommodate her computer setup and a typewriter, a wicker love seat with a bright print cushion and several bookcases that groaned with the burden of the books she had accumulated over a lifetime of reading, researching and writing. Flowers and growing things were everywhere, from the floral still-life prints on the walls to a miniature bouquet of china roses on her desk and a rack of potted plants in front of the long, narrow window.

Charity turned on her computer and instructed it to format a disk, preparing it to receive the information she and Lance would punch into the keyboard. The computer had just begun emitting the electronic squeaks and whirs that attended the process when the doorbell rang.

She had thought all her nervousness would dissipate as soon as she saw Lance. She had thought that she would smile and say hello, and he would say hello, and everything would be normal again. She had thought they would sit down and work as though they'd never been locked in a car trunk together and hadn't kissed each other as though they'd both just been rescued from separate islands where they'd spent years without having seen another member of the opposite sex.

The moment Lance stepped into her living room, she knew that she had been mistaken.

Charity did not like pop psychology or media catch-phrases, but she understood implicitly the meaning of the phrase, "having one's space invaded." Surrounded by the airy, distinctly feminine ambience of her apart-ment, Lance—large, strong and distinctly male—was an alien presence. And Charity had never been more aware of the difference between men and women in her life, nor more aware of the significance of that difference. How could she have been so naive as to think they'd just pretend the kiss never happened—or that they could just ignore the force that had led them into the kiss in the first place?

He was in her apartment, as incongruous as the proverbial bull in the china shop, and she was standing in the middle of the floor staring at him, being stared at by him, and wondering what the hell she was supposed to *say* to him. She swallowed and unconsciously ran the tip of her tongue over her lips to moisten them.

"Did you have any problem finding my apartment?" she asked, and silently breathed out a sigh of relief. The question was, if not brilliant, at least appropriate and coherent. It sounded almost like normal, casual, everyday conversation.

"No," Lance said, distractedly. He was looking around the room, and she suddenly saw it through his eyes, all chintz and ruffles and touches of lace. He must feel as though he'd stumbled into a life-size doll's house.

So what am I supposed to do—apologize for being me? she thought bitterly, feeling exposed and disapproved of. Long seconds passed, and she reminded herself that it was her turn to speak. Lord, but dealing with him had been easier before they *liked* each other. There was a time when she wouldn't have cared what he thought of her decor.

"Would you like a cup of coffee?" she asked. He nodded and followed her into the cheery kitchen. She poured the coffee and turned to find Lance studying the kitchen witch on her wall with absorbed interest.

It was a comic figurine, sculpted from nylon stockings, that she'd bought at a sidewalk art show. The distinguishing feature of this witch was that she rode her miniature broom without a stitch of clothes on. It was a rear view, and the witch's white, cotton-candy hair splayed wildly over her back to her waist, stopping just above her plump and dimpled buttocks.

The small tag hanging from the broom handle identified the witch as Brunhilde Bottoms. Charity had thought the entire Bottoms family clever and irreverent and cute. *Must have been a moment of madness,* she thought now. "They're supposed to be good luck," she said defensively, wishing she'd never gone to that stupid art show.

"They?" Lance said, eyeing the dual globes of Brunhilde Bottoms's backside dubiously.

"Kitchen witches," she said.

Lance's "Oh" was astoundingly communicative.

The china pedestal mug she handed him looked absurdly delicate in his big hand, and she was struck again by the inappropriateness of his being there. He simply didn't fit. He was too large, out of proportion. She'd had a number of male visitors in her apartment—friends, boyfriends, husbands of friends—but Lance was the first one that had ever made her so overwhelmingly aware of his presence that her comfortable, familiar rooms seemed crowded.

The situation grew even more acute as they entered the short, narrow hallway that led to her office. As he walked closely behind her, she felt the heat of his fit body and remembered the way that body had felt against hers. What she wanted most in the whole world to do now was stop, turn around and let herself be wrapped in his manly warmth again.

The paddle ceiling fan whirled into motion when she switched on the light, and she was grateful for the surge of air it forced across her face. Oxygen seemed in short supply in the close confines of the office walls.

"I, uh, there's only one chair behind the desk, but I thought maybe one of the dinette chairs would fit...." The expression on Lance's face stopped her. Very gently he took the cup from her hand and set it on the corner of her desk next to his own.

He put his hands on her arms, loosely encircling the tops of them with his fingers. "We can't ignore it," he said. "We can't pretend it never happened."

She understood what he was saying and, swallowing to moisten her dry throat, nodded. Lance moved a step closer to her, and anticipation stole her breath away. He raised one hand to brush her hair away from her face, and his thumb stroked lightly over her cheek.

His gentle smile was in direct opposition to the savageness of the emotions thundering inside Charity. Very slowly he lowered his head and brushed his lips over hers, lightly, tentatively. Charity gasped involuntarily at the sensuous tickle of his breath on her skin and stood on tiptoe to reestablish the contact with his lips. Her arms slid up over his shoulders to draw him close to her, and she parted her lips as the kiss deepened in urgency and intensity.

Ending such intimacy abruptly was unthinkable. When Lance lifted his lips from hers, Charity pressed a trail of tiny kisses on Lance's cheeks before moving lower to nibble at the sturdy cords of his neck. Lance inhaled sharply and tightened his arms around her. An unspoken understanding passed between them: it stops here, or it doesn't stop at all.

Charity sighed reluctantly and nestled her cheek against his chest and listened to the rushing beat of his heart. Lance propped his chin comfortably on the top of her head, and when his breathing had slowed to normal, said, "Maybe we can get some work done now that we've got that over with."

Charity laughed into the broad wall of muscles that crisscrossed his chest. Lance might not be a romantic, but he had an uncanny instinct for defusing awkward situations. She could picture him coolly talking desperate felons into surrendering their weapons or releasing hostages in dead-end situations. *Or charming a snake out of its rattles,* she thought with a shiver that was part delight and part apprehension. He wasn't exactly botching the job of charming *her*.

Lifting her head away from his chest, she grinned up at him. "Now that we've got that over with, I guess we'd better try. Get a chair from the other room, and I'll finish setting up the computer." When he returned and plopped the chair down next to hers, she said, "I named the file Synopsis for now. You haven't come up with any ideas for a title for this great American novel we're writing, have you?"

"Not yet. I thought we should play on the diary angle somehow."

"I agree. I came up with *Madame's Diary*, but it just doesn't conjure up the right mood. We want to project adventure and intrigue and maybe a little glamour." She shrugged. "Oh, well, we've got plenty of time to worry about the title. How do we open the synopsis?"

"At the beginning?" Lance suggested.

Charity's fingers flew over the keyboard, and she read aloud as the words appeared on the screen: "Attorney Shea Tremaine is called to the jail when..."

"How about beautiful attorney?" Lance suggested.

"How about voluptuous?"

"Yes," Lance agreed. "Voluptuous is good."

Three hours later, they were only halfway through their notes. After taking a shift at the keyboard, Lance had given up on the hard dinette chair and was dividing his time between pacing in the limited space of the office and sprawling what he could fit of his long frame over the wicker love seat.

A startled cry of, "What the...?" drew Charity's startled attention just in time to see Lance come close to karate chopping her cat in a purely reflexive reaction to having an orange beast leap upon his chest and dig in its talons. Stopping himself in the nick of time, he glared at Charity accusingly over the bristled hairs on O.J.'s back. "Friend of yours?" he asked with a fair share of rage.

Charity chuckled. "I should have warned you. The love seat is O.J.'s favorite resting spot. I take it he dug in his claws when he landed."

"Front and rear," Lance said dryly.

"You surprised him."

"We're even, then. He surprised me. Does your liability coverage extend to a wild-animal attack?"

"I've got some peroxide in the medicine chest," she said. "I could..."

"Never mind," he grumbled, and then, eyeing O.J. skeptically, he said, "*This* is your cat?"

"I'm not the kind of girl who has stray tomcats lying around on her love seat," she quipped.

"I thought...oh, never mind. What am I supposed to do about him?"

"Well, you could push him onto the floor, but that hardly seems sporting, since technically it's his love seat by prior possession. Or you could pet him, in which case he'll promptly go to sleep on your chest." She let her shoulders sag against the high back of the executive-style desk chair and exhaled wearily. "Or, since we're at the end of a scene, you could pet him politely then leave him on the love seat to snooze while we break for lunch."

"Splendid idea. My stomach's been grumbling for half an hour."

Charity glared at him exasperatedly. "Why didn't you say something?"

"We were getting a lot done." Lance gingerly unfolded from the love seat and settled O.J. onto the cushion. He walked around the desk to where Charity was now standing, absently rubbing her taut neck muscles. Pushing her hands away, he resumed the kneading motion with his experienced fingers.

"Mmmm," Charity said, the word close to a sigh. "There are real advantages to this collaboration stuff."

Lance leaned forward and, poking his head over her shoulder, kissed her cheek. "I'm going to demand equal time with this treatment one of these days."

"Willingly granted," Charity said, guilelessly relaxing her shoulders against the warmth of his chest. "Just don't stop."

"Want an all-over alcohol rubdown?"

When she stepped out of his reach and scowled at him playfully, he shrugged and said, "I figured you wouldn't. What's for lunch?"

"Fettuccine primavera."

"Unfair! You promised not to fuss."

"It's just a fancy name for vegetables with noodles. Store-bought noodles, at that."

"Is there any other kind?"

"I make them fresh for special occasions. But I don't have a fettuccine blade on my noodle machine."

Lance slung his arm across her shoulders as they walked, and whispered suggestively into her ear, "I've never a known a woman with a noodle machine. Will you show me yours sometime?"

His slightly naughty mood was contagious. "Right after I show you my private collection of art prints," she answered.

"I just remembered something," Lance said, taking his arm from around her and racing ahead of her down the hall.

"What is it?" she called after him, nonplussed.

He had stopped in the kitchen and grinned at her sadistically when she reached the door. Wringing his hands like a villain in a bad horror movie, he laughed diabolically and, feigning madness, turned toward the refrigerator. "I'm going to look inside."

Charity flung herself between him and the refrigerator and covered her face with the backs of her hands, cringing, and managed to say, before bursting into giggles, "No, no, not that. Anything but that."

"Out of the way," he said, gently nudging her aside. "No drawer is sacred, no shelf is beyond the range of my scrutiny."

"Please," she said, still with one hand to her forehead, "be gentle."

He opened the door with a dramatic yank, took one look and then turned his full attention to Charity. "You did this on purpose."

"Well," she hedged, and then confessed, "I might have cleaned it recently."

"What did you do, use paste wax on the walls?"

"It's not *that* clean."

"A doctor could perform open-heart surgery in there."

"Without a single case of salmonella contagion," she pointed out.

Lance ignored her. "Soy sauce, Worcestershire sauce. What's this? Good grief. Who keeps garlic in the refrigerator?"

"People who like fresh garlic."

"I like your little garlic-shaped bowl. It's so *cute*."

Temptation overwhelmed her; she picked up a towel from the counter and walloped him with it. The blow was totally ineffectual. "You didn't have to get sarcastic. It's a garlic cellar."

"There are holes in it."

"Garlic has to breathe."

"Congratulations, Ms. Lovejoy," Lance said wryly. "You're refrigerator's not only clean, it's vampire proof."

"Feeling weak, Count Palmer?"

"Yes. Transfusion time!" he cried, and with a lightning-quick fluid movement, trapped her in his arms and nibbled noisily at her neck.

Charity's laughter dissolved into a mellow sigh as the game turned from funny to serious. Lance lifted his head to look at her face, and their eyes locked. She held her breath as she waited, unresisting, for him to kiss her.

A woman like Charity can't be rushed. Lance heard the echo of his own words haunting him, wishing he could deny the wisdom in them. When she looked the way she looked now—her eyes half closed, her lips slightly parted in an enigmatic half smile—he *wanted* to rush her. He wanted to crush her into his arms and forget finesse and propriety and simply *feel*.

He settled for kissing her gently on the lips and then dropping a parting kiss, studiously casual, on her forehead before turning back to the refrigerator. "What's in the crisper drawer?"

"Most of what we need for lunch," Charity said, glad her voice sounded normal. The kiss had been devastating through its very gentleness. "As long as you're probing and prodding, dig out the zucchini, a green pepper, an onion, that little sprig of broccoli and the carton of mushrooms."

Lance gathered the vegetables and set them on the counter. "I thought you said this was simple."

"Trust me," she said. "The most complicated job is getting the noodles *al dente*."

"What can I do to help?"

"I'm not sure I trust you with a knife in the mood you're in. Why don't you watch this water and drop the noodles in when it starts to boil." She washed the vegetables and began chopping.

"Don't you know that watched pots never boil?" he asked after half a minute of staring at the pot and feeling like a fool. "It's a rule or something."

"It's an old proverb with no basis in scientific fact. However, if you're too antsy to watch it, then you can slice while I cook."

"Oh, I'm trusted with a knife now?"

"I'm feeling reckless." *In more ways than one,* she thought wryly.

Like all the rooms in the apartment, the kitchen was small. She and Lance were scarcely four feet apart as they worked, yet Lance no longer seemed so much like a giant invading her home.

What a difference a few hours make—what a difference a *kiss* makes, Charity thought. Without being overly analytical, she acknowledged and accepted the fact that the nature of their relationship had changed with that second kiss. They were no longer simply collaborators, professionals linked together by complementary talents. They were a man and a woman who worked well together, enjoyed each other's company and found each other sexually attractive.

Lance had demonstrated his complacency with the change through an attitude of casual acceptance, and his nonchalance smoothed the path for a similar acceptance on her behalf.

They bantered through lunch, laughing, teasing, enjoying each other's company, and carried the same comfortable familiarity back into Charity's office as they resumed their work.

Hours passed before they finally reached the last page of their notes. Lance typed The End onto the screen, reading the words aloud. Charity was in the chair next to him and he put his hand on her knee in a familiar, chummy gesture and smiled. "Let's store this baby and find a good steak house." Noting the surprise that skittered across her face, he said, "You don't have previous plans, do you?"

"No," she admitted.

"Then come on. We deserve a break after all that hard work."

"You talked me into it," she said. "Just give me five minutes."

Five minutes—she spent five frantic minutes in the bathroom freshening her makeup, brushing her hair and dusting on perfumed talc. Lance had called the upcoming dinner out a deserved break, but it felt like an old-fashioned boy-girl date. Charity had butterflies of anticipation flapping their wings in her stomach to prove it.

The evening, in fact, progressed exactly in that vein. They talked about everything and nothing, about fishing and publishers, about alligators and the eagles that nested near Aripeka. Having bypassed the awkward what's-your-name, what-do-you-do phase, they had slid into that enchanted period of courtship when every discovery of the other was exciting, every moment in each other's company exhilarating. They talked, they laughed, they held hands under the table.

And, like all enchanted evenings, it ended in the gentlest, most exciting of good-night kisses, just before Lance disappeared into the night.

Chapter Seven

You're the expert on jails," Charity said to Lance. "Where would an attorney consult with her client? Would she go into the cell, or are there interview rooms?"

They were seated on the deck at Lance's house the next day, jotting detailed notes on a yellow legal pad.

"It depends on the jail," Lance said. "It could be either."

"I vote for the interview room. What would it look like?"

"Bleak. Institutional gray walls. A battered table and uncomfortable wooden chairs. A guard at the door."

"Good details," Charity said, scribbling furiously. "Shea can be waiting there for them to bring Carlotta in."

"What do you think of *The Carlotta Chronicles* for a title?" Lance asked.

"*The Carlotta Chronicles*," Charity repeated. "The cadence is right. And I like the alliteration. Let's use it as the working title. If we come up with something catchier by the time we finish the three chapters, we can always change it. *The Carlotta Chronicles*. Has a good ring to it."

"I thought so," Lance said. "I was going over synonyms for diary and came up with chronicle, and then when I put Carlotta and chronicle together—well, as you said, the alliteration is good. But the cadence was wrong in *Carlotta's Chronicles*, so the next logical progression was to drop the apostrophe and add *the*."

"The more I hear it, the better I like it," Charity said. "Now all we have to do is decide whether the byline should be Lance Palmer and Charity Lovejoy or Charity Lovejoy and Lance Palmer."

Lance scoffed at the notion of a battle for top billing. "We could always put Tony on the spot and make him decide."

"It would serve him right if we made him think we've got a real feud brewing over it," Charity said.

"You know Tony," Lance said. "He'd come up with something like, 'Standard procedure is to arrange them alphabetically,' or find some other way to slide out from under the burden of decision."

"You're probably right. That's probably exactly what he'd do. Still, it might be fun to make him sweat over it awhile."

"Are you still miffed at Tony for roping you into this collaboration?" Lance said, his eyes settling on her face as he waited for an answer.

Charity didn't flinch away from that probing search for a frank answer. "I was never miffed," she said, her eyes meeting his evenly. "I was wary. But Tony was right, as usual. The man's instincts are infallible."

"Especially when he smells money," Lance reminded her, and they laughed. Following a brief, unstrained silence, Lance turned that intense gaze on her face again. "I'm glad he bullied me into it," he said solemnly.

Charity's breath caught in her throat, and she had to pause before answering, "So am I."

This time the silence was significant. And long. Finally, Charity poised her pen over the legal pad. "We left attorney Shea Tremaine in the interview room waiting for Carlotta. The guard brings Carlotta in. What's she wearing? Would she have on a prison smock yet?"

The abrupt question effectively switched the gears of their focus from personal back to business. So far they'd been very successful at keeping the two segments of their relationship separate, and both understood it was absolutely essential that they continue to do so. So, after having admitted that they were glad they were working together, they proceeded to work together until the sound of an automobile engine and the telltale squeak of brakes broke their concentration. Tilly sprang to attention and loped to the edge of the deck and growled menacingly. The engine revved slightly and then the mechanical sound of it faded gradually.

"That's my mail," Lance said. "Mind if we break long enough for me to check the box?"

"Not at all," Charity said. "It's sacrilege for a writer to leave mail in a box more than thirty seconds."

She stood up and rolled her shoulders to work out the kinks of inactivity as Lance, with Tilly dancing at his heels, walked off in the direction of the mailbox. She was nonplussed when a glance at her wristwatch revealed they'd been working nearly two hours. No wonder she was stiff.

"Fan mail?" she asked, when Lance returned and settled into his chair with the stack of envelopes in his lap.

"From the electric company," Lance said, recognizing the distinctive logo on one of the envelopes. "They write once a month to tell me how much they enjoy the checks I write them."

"I hear from them regularly, too," Charity said.

"American Express loves me, too," Lance said, still shuffling through the stack of mail. An envelope of buff-colored linen-weave stationery caught his eye, and he stared at it with perceivable hesitation before opening it.

Feeling uncomfortable in the role of voyeur as he read his personal mail, Charity said, "I'm going to get a glass of water." Lance nodded distractedly, but didn't look up. Charity went into the house and took her time sipping the water until Lance came inside and laid some of the mail on the counter and tossed the junk mail into the trash can.

On top of the stack of keepers, there was a photograph of a child in a baseball uniform. He was grinning at the camera self-consciously, and his two front teeth were missing, so he looked part elf, part urchin. Since Lance had laid the photograph in plain sight, Charity did not feel she was meddling by looking at it. "What a darling child," she said.

Lance's words were heavy as stones. "That's my son."

For several protracted seconds, Charity just stared at him, stupefied. Then, regaining her senses, she said, hoarsely, "I didn't know you had children."

"Just the one," Lance said. "And he's not mine any more, really." His pain was a poignant, almost tangible thing.

Charity laid her hand on his arm to comfort him. "You don't have to tell me about it, but I'll listen if you want to."

Lance stared at her hand a moment and then covered it with his own, accepting the comfort she offered. His eyes sought hers, held them as he spoke. "My ex-wife, Katy, remarried shortly after he was born, and her husband adopted him. He doesn't even have my name." His ragged sigh, so impregnated with pain and guilt, cut at Charity's heart. "I didn't want to give him up. I said no to the adoption at first, but—"

He drew in a fortifying breath before continuing. "Her husband was there, living with him, being his father anyway. He could give Bobby everything I couldn't. Even if I'd packed up and moved to Indiana, I couldn't have been a full-time father to him when I didn't live with him. Katy thought it would be less confusing to Bobby if he had the same last name as she did, so I did what was best for the boy."

He picked up the photograph and they both studied it. Charity could see the resemblance between father and son in the shape of the nose and something around the eyes, and she realized the resemblance would've been obvious immediately if not for the scars on Lance's face.

"He's going to visit me when he's old enough to understand that he can have a biological father and a legal father, too. It was part of the adoption arrangement.

For now, Katy sends pictures, and I write letters and send him presents on his birthday and at Christmas. He just knows they come from a friend named Lance Palmer.''

He shook his head and a sound that was pure bitterness rose from his throat. ''You've heard of surrogate mothers? Here's a case of a surrogate father. It's all been very civilized. Katy's husband was a high-powered attorney, and now he's a judge. A judge, for God's sake. Can't get more civilized than that. Hell, the biggest favor I ever did my son was divorcing his mother so she could marry the embodiment of the American way.''

Charity touched his cheek with her fingertips, drawing his attention to her own face. ''You're being too hard on yourself. If it didn't work out between you and...'' She didn't want to give the shadowy figure from his past a name; ascribing a name to his ex-wife gave her a credibility in the present, and Charity didn't want his ex-wife between them. She slid her arms around Lance's waist and hugged him, nestling her cheek against his chest. ''There was no way you could be a full-time father to him,'' she said. ''You did what was best for your son, no matter what it cost you.''

Cost you. The words triggered comprehension. She had heard the story before—she had *read* the story, or at least the beginning of it, before. Too stunned for tact, she blurted bluntly, ''You're Charlie in *The Cost of Being a Cop*, aren't you?''

He nodded silently, telling her yes through the gentle movement of his chin against her scalp.

''I didn't know,'' she said. ''I never suspected. I knew they were true case histories, but I didn't know it was autobiographical.''

"No one knew, outside of my close friends in the department," Lance said. "It was a legal understanding with the publisher. My role in the story was not to be revealed or exploited in any way. Can you imagine what a circus it would have been if people had known? Lord, if they'd found Bobby, he'd have been in the center ring."

"And the story of Charlie's marriage and divorce— that was how it was between you and—" this time she couldn't avoid the name "—Katy?"

"Yes."

Charity closed her eyes, absorbing the new knowledge about him, the new understanding of his attitude toward love and marriage. "No wonder those passages were so poignant."

"The police psychiatrist said writing the story was very therapeutic. Catharsis was the word he used."

Catharsis or no catharsis, it was evident to Charity that Lance was nowhere close to putting his failed marriage and his lost child behind him. It didn't take a psychiatrist to identify symptoms of unresolved pain, guilt and bitterness in his attitude.

At least he'd gotten through the acceptance phase, she thought. It was obvious he accepted Katy's second marriage as a fait accompli and didn't harbor any hopes that Katy might walk in the door holding their son by the hand and ask if they could try to make it as a family again. No wonder he was so cynical about love and romance. His large, strong body camouflaged emotional scars far more debilitating than the scars that marred the perfection of his face.

Involuntarily she tightened her arms around his waist, moving closer to him in an instinctive urge to console him for the general unfairness of life. How sad the entire situation was for him.

And, she realized suddenly as she felt his arms go around her and his hands come to rest on her back, how dangerous it was for her. She was in imminent danger of falling in love with him.

Danger and differing philosophies were the last thing on Lance's mind at the moment. He was thinking how sweet it was to have Charity snuggled next to him and enjoying the feel of her in his arms, the human warmth of her body against his, the firm pressure of her breasts against his upper ribs.

For nearly six years he'd been getting terse letters with photographs in them from Katy, but this was the first time he'd ever let anyone give him a feel-better hug after he'd received one.

It came as a shock to him to realize that he had deliberately left the photograph where she could see it, hoping she would ask who it was. He could easily have tucked the photo back into the envelope, but he'd left it in plain sight. He had *wanted* to tell her about Bobby. Had he sensed that she would understand him, comfort him, tell him not to be so hard on himself? He didn't know. He wasn't even sure he wanted to know, because he didn't want to deal with the possible implications. All he wanted to think about was that she was there and it felt good to have her hug him and tell him he'd done the right thing. In fact, he couldn't remember the last time he'd felt so relieved to have confided in someone—or when holding a woman had seemed so right.

They stood there, arms around each other, for several minutes, before Charity made the first move to withdraw from the embrace. Lifting her head from his chest, she said, "We have a book to write."

Lance threaded his fingers into her hair and kissed her temple. "Let's play hooky instead."

Having his fingers curled around the contours of her scalp caressingly was all the persuasion she needed to let her cheek rest against his chest again and ask, "What did you have in mind?"

He kissed the top of her head. "There's only one genuine, American way to play hooky. You said you have a license, didn't you?"

Thirty minutes later they were leaving the beer and bait with a bucket of mullets; they had sandwiches, potato chips and six-packs of cola and beer, which Lance put in the ice chest and covered with ice.

"I'm supposed to be teaching you good work habits, but you're corrupting me," Charity said. "We really needed to work today."

"The beauty of writing is that it can be done anywhere," Lance replied. "You brought your notebook, didn't you?"

"Yes, but..."

"We can talk just as easily on the pier as we can sitting on the deck. We'll alternate with the rod, and one of us can take notes."

"There's a hole in that theory somewhere," Charity said with a smile, "but I'm not real keen on finding it. Just the idea of playing hooky gives you a delicious sense of getting away with something, doesn't it?"

"Um-hm," he agreed.

"I never skipped school when I was growing up," she said.

"Not even once?"

"Protestant work ethic, I guess," she said, shrugging her shoulders. "In addition to the absolute knowledge that my parents would cream me if they ever found out. It's called discipline by intimidation. I don't know what I thought they'd *do* actually, but I was sure that if I skipped class, they'd find out and something *terrible* would happen."

"I tried it once in fourth grade and got caught. My mother made me write, 'I will not skip school,' a hundred times."

His *mother*, not his dad, she thought. "Were your parents divorced?" she said.

"My dad died when I was seven."

"I'm sorry," Charity said. She couldn't imagine what it would have been like growing up without both parents. Her parents had been extremely busy, always a team, always preoccupied with the problems of the church and the congregation. Sometimes she'd felt she was part of that parabolic flock of one hundred, instead of one of two children, but, like the one lost sheep, she could always depend on one of her parents to listen to her and nurture her when she needed nurturing. They even joked about it together sometimes. How awful it must have been for a boy growing up without a father.

"He was killed in a shoot-out at a liquor-store robbery."

"He was a cop?"

Lance nodded. "They gave him a medal for heroism—posthumously. I went up on the stage with my mother to get it, and everyone shook my hand, as though I was a grown-up instead of a child, and told me how proud I should be of him."

"Is that why you became a cop?"

"I picked up the gauntlet," he said flatly. "It never occurred to me I could do anything else."

"That must have made it doubly hard for you to quit."

"Yes, it did," Lance said, impressed by her perception. Charity Lovejoy, he reflected, would be a difficult woman to keep a secret from—not that he had any secrets left to keep from her.

The pier where Lance always fished was deserted except for a solitary pelican perched on the railing at the far end who eyed them warily as they approached, but seemed to decide they were harmless when they didn't move beyond the center point and, having thus decided, didn't bother to fly away. "Do you suppose he's an undercover truant officer?" Charity asked, when the bird continued staring at them.

"Probably on Tony's payroll," Lance replied dryly, and Charity giggled.

After they finished their sandwiches, Lance baited both their hooks and they sat side by side, dangling their legs from the pier and waiting for some action. And they waited. Twenty minutes later something grabbed Lance's line and set his reel whirring, but after a fight, whatever it was swam away, having made a free dinner of the bait. Lance cursed and reeled in his line. "Better check yours," he said. "Some of these fish are so crafty they steal bait without even bobbing the hook."

She reeled in her line, and sure enough, the bait was no longer on her hook. Lance took her rod when she said, "Don't bait it again. I think I'll get my notebook so we can plot the scene where the psychiatrist's men see her going in after the diary."

Lance gave her his rod, already baited. "Toss this one out, and I'll get the notebook."

He returned and instead of sitting beside her, settled behind her, straddling her hips and thighs with his long legs. Laying the notebook on a wood plank, he slipped his arms around her and crossed them over her waist in front of her. They fit snugly between the top of her thighs and the bottom of her breasts. When he began nibbling on her earlobe, Charity said, "I'm not sure this is the kind of work we're supposed to be doing."

"You're just letting Agent Double-O-Fishbreath intimidate you," he said, with a wave toward the nearby pelican, who was still eyeing them contemptuously.

"I don't think he's the one intimidating me," she said, casting a glance at the bird.

"Don't tell me I'm making you nervous," Lance said.

"You realize that if I get a big fish, we could both wind up in the drink?"

"I'll hold on to you."

"You're already holding on to me." He was, in fact, holding her quite securely and, while she knew she should be discouraging such intimacy, she just plain didn't want to push him away. Instead, she recklessly allowed her shoulders to relax against his chest and sighed. Lance rested his chin on her shoulder blade and said, "Playing hooky wasn't this much fun in the fourth grade."

"That's because you hadn't discovered girls yet."

He nuzzled her hair out of the way and kissed the sensitive area just in front of her ear. "Maybe it was because I hadn't discovered *you* yet."

"What an incredibly sweet thing to say," she murmured, leaning her head into the crook of his shoulder. Strange, wonderful sensations were radiating through her. He was so close to her, his body so solid and warm and substantial where it touched hers. Even the inescapable knowledge that he found her desirable did not embarrass her because their intimacy was such a comfortable one.

This is what I write about, she thought, *this kind of closeness and oneness of mind and spirit.* It was a sobering realization. She had always dreamed of falling in love, but Lance Palmer wasn't the type of man she'd dreamed of falling in love with. He was too physical, too cynical, too emotionally bruised. Yet she couldn't deny the emotions being near him evoked in her. It was not merely a physical reaction to his unadulterated manliness, it was an emotional attraction as well. She liked his wry humor, his way of saying sweet things at unexpected moments, the fact that he was sure enough of himself to admit that he could learn from her, the way he listened to her.

And, she had to admit, she absolutely adored the way he was nibbling on her earlobe. But he was going to be nibbling on a lot more if she didn't do something to stop this assault on her senses, and she knew she had to do something about it. She was trying to decide what when the matter was settled by the sudden loud wheezing of the fishing line being reeled out. The yank on the rod made her jerk to attention and start pumping the rod and reeling in the fish.

Lance raised his hands, ready to take the rod, but seeing that Charity handled it proficiently, he wrapped his arms loosely around her waist again. "You really do know how to fish," he said incredulously.

"This one's a fighter," she said, slightly winded by the battle in progress. "What do you think it is?"

Lance took his right arm from around her and lifted her hair from the nape of her neck and kissed the tender area there. "Could be anything. Is the drag okay?"

"It'll have to do. Can't adjust it now or we'll lose him."

Lance gingerly extricated his body from around her, saying, "I'll get the net ready." Absorbed in the fight, Charity only nodded.

"You would think," he observed wryly, "that Moby Dick is on the line."

"You said it could be anything," she said, straining to control the rod.

Amused by her true land-it-or-die fisherman's attitude, Lance grinned. She probably wouldn't want to hear about how cute he thought she was with that scowl of concentration knitting her brow, but she couldn't prevent him thinking it. Watching her struggle, it was difficult for him not to offer to take over the rod and the battle, but he bit back the urge. It was her fish; she'd either land it or lose it. "Hands off, unless asked" was an unwritten fisherman's creed that he respected as much as she did.

It took over a quarter of an hour for her to get the fish out of the water, and it still had enough fight to tax Lance's considerable skill with the net. "What kind is it?" Charity asked.

"Redfish," Lance said. "Haven't caught one of these in a while."

"It's not Moby Dick," Charity said, able now to get her first close look at the catch, "but it's not exactly Moby Minnow, either."

"It's big enough to make dinner for two tonight," Lance said.

Readying himself for a refusal, he was preparing to coax her into it when she said, "I don't clean them." When he didn't reply, she said more emphatically, "I catch fish, but I don't *touch* them when they're flopping around staring at me. And I don't cut them open and *gut* them. So unless you're volunteering..."

With a rumble of male laughter, Lance said, "I love a woman who knows the difference between man's work and woman's work."

"I hate to disillusion you and pop that chauvinistic bubble, but I'm afraid I don't know how to cook redfish, either." An irritating grin spread over his face. Defensively, she said, "I'm a good cook, really. I do okay with flounder and trout. I've just never handled redfish before."

Lance patted her on the head as he would a child or a puppy, and said, in a condescending tone of voice, "Don't worry, sweetheart. The only proper way to cook redfish is Cajun style, and that's man's cooking."

"Do women get to eat it, too, or do they just stand around waiting to wash the dishes after the men have finished?"

Laughing, Lance slung his arm across her shoulders and hugged her broadly. "You caught it, sweetheart. I could hardly let you starve to death." He paused just long enough to let her know he was teasing. "You can have the leftovers when I'm finished."

"No way!" she said, playfully pummeling his chest with her fist. "I'll just take my fish and find someone else to clean it and cook it."

He caught her wrist in midswing and held it suspended in air between them. "Please don't," he said, his eyes fixed on her face. All the teasing had gone from his voice.

But not from Charity's. In an effort to lighten the sudden seriousness of the moment, she said, "You just want my redfish."

Lance followed her lead. "True. My mouth started watering for blackened redfish the moment I saw it come out of the water. But good company will make it taste even better. You'll stay?"

She nodded. "But only because I want to see if you really know how to cook. After seeing your refrigerator..."

"You'll see," he said, and after applying a playful swat to her backside, proceeded with the chore of putting the fish on the stringer. Charity watched perplexedly as he lowered the stringer into the water and secured it and wondered why she wasn't even mildly annoyed at the liberty he'd taken and why an affectionate pat on the fanny seemed quite natural and proper between them. She'd directed withering scowls at a number of men for trying the same familiarity.

Lance baited the hook again and offered the rod to Charity, preparing to bait the second one.

"No, thanks," she said. "I've pulled off my coup for the day." She had settled Indian-style on the pier with the notebook in her lap. "Now," she said, as Lance sat down and cast his line into the water, "about the scene where the psychiatrist's men see her go in after the diary..."

They stayed at the pier another two hours and wound up getting a lot more done on their manuscript than on adding to supper. Though Lance fished continuously, the activity on the end of his line gave no indication that any of the billions of fish residing in the murky depths of the Gulf of Mexico were cavorting anywhere near

Aripeka, nor that any who were were hungry for mullet purchased from the beer and bait.

In the end, Charity gingerly picked up the mullets by the tail and flung them to the pelican, who mustered a dignified enthusiasm for them. "How are you at roasting pelican?" Lance quipped wryly, abandoning his pole and tiptoeing toward the bird with his net in hand.

"Lance!" she cried, so outraged that he spun around and walked toward her instead of the pelican and, dropping the net, threw his arms around her and hugged her so tight that he lifted her feet off the pier. Surprised, she squealed, and he laughed aloud, a deep, resonant, feel-good belly laugh of pure joy that carried over the water, and then faded into a sigh of contentment as he lowered her gradually until her feet met the wooden surface again. "Toss Double-O the rest of the bait and let's go. I want to show you how a *man* cooks."

Later, at his house, she leaned against the counter next to the gas range and watched Lance supervise the heating of an iron skillet. It was, she observed skeptically, hot enough for any practical purpose short of causing a meltdown of the polar ice caps and was producing a thin thread of smoke. "Are you trying to burn the house down to keep me from finding out you can't cook?" she teased.

Lance assumed a pose of arrogant superiority. "You think so? Well, that just goes to show how much you don't know about blackened redfish. Technically the skillet should be heated until it's white hot, but that's not practical on a home stove, so we'll settle for hot as blue blazes. Now, step back, please, so you don't get splattered, and watch the master."

"Your house is going to smell like fish for a week," she called to him through a haze of smoke as the filets sizzled. She was certain he was burning them, and was prepared to be kind about it, but when she tasted the final product—crisp on the outside, soft in the middle and saucy as the vocabulary of a sailor's parrot—she was forced to admit it was not only edible but delicious.

"I'm not one to say I told you so, but I, uh, told you so," Lance said with a smug cat-who-swallowed-the-canary grin.

"Just to show you how contrite I am over doubting you," she said, "I'll do the dishes."

She washed and Lance dried until the only dirty dish left was the still-warm iron skillet that was as blackened as the redfish cooked in it. "Just fill it with warm soapy water," Lance said. "I'll scour and season it later."

Charity smiled at him gratefully. "I was hoping you'd say that." Then, after setting the pan to soak, she washed her hands and dried them on the towel he was holding.

Lance captured her right hand before she could pull it away and drew it to his cheek, rubbing the soft skin on the back of it against the roughness of a day's growth of beard and then brushing her fingertips across his lips. "Stay awhile?" he asked. "We could work, or play cards or..."

It was the last, unspoken possibility that prompted Charity to answer, "I can't. It's already pitch dark outside, and it's a long drive home."

A chill had settled over the night, and Charity shivered as she stepped into the breeze. Lance put his arm across her shoulder and rubbed the top of her arm with his palm. "Spring isn't quite as close as we thought."

"I guess not."

They kissed good-night briefly, gently, sweetly, and then Lance watched Charity drive off into the black night and wished he could at least have seen her home safely. Was it training, he wondered, all the times his mother had drilled into him that he didn't leave his date without making sure she was safely inside her home, or was it some innate protective instinct Charity nudged to life within him? Probably a little of both, he decided, although a little less of the former and a little more of the latter.

Charity, he admitted wryly to himself, seemed to be triggering a lot of reactions and instincts in him. He hadn't wanted her to leave at all. He had wanted to keep on kissing her, to move his lips upward from her fingers, to her palm and the inside crook of her elbow and then her shoulders, those soft, narrow shoulders, and then her neck. He had wanted to hold her as he'd held her earlier and feel the entire length of her body against him and then to discover her, peeling off her clothes inch by inch, and then let her discover him the same way. And then he would have carried her to bed and made passionate love to her.

But his desire hadn't been as simple as that, because his fantasy included holding her next to him afterward and talking to her in the still darkness and then falling asleep with her nestled against him. It wasn't simply a fantasy of having sex but one of making love, which was something quite different, and the scope of it had shaken him sufficiently to let her leave without trying to persuade her to stay.

Chapter Eight

One of these days you're going to open your mouth to meow and an oink is going to come out," Charity warned O.J. He had greeted her at the door with an outraged meow and led her directly to the kitchen, where he alternated between staring at his food dish expectantly and meowing his displeasure over her having been remiss enough to let it get empty.

Charity filled the dish and then, as the cat attacked the fresh food, returned to the living room, where she kicked off her shoes, put her favorite tape on the stereo and settled on the sofa to read the day's mail.

It was fairly routine: a bill, a slick sales catalog from a local department store, a letter from her parents. She slid her finger under the flap of the familiar blue bond envelope and opened it, but hesitated before taking out the folded letter, suddenly remembering the buff-colored envelope in Lance's stack of mail and the expression of staid anticipation on his face as he'd stared at it, an expression so explicit that it had prompted her to leave him alone so he could read it in private.

She heaved a deep sigh of empathy for him, for the situation in which he was inexorably muddled. Those buff-colored envelopes must be instruments of torture to him; opening them would be like tearing open an old wound. How awful it must be for him to look at his son's face, feeling first the surge of pride and then the inevitable, creeping awareness that the child called another man Daddy.

With another sigh, she unfolded the letter from her mother and read the benign, familiar revelation of events in the lives of the Lovejoy family, immediate and distant. Great-aunt Hope was still hoping to organize a family reunion during the summer. No surprise in that, Charity thought. Great-aunt Hope couldn't stand having kith and kin scattered across the country because it made butting into everyone's business so inconvenient.

Charity's parents were considering taking a cruise in late summer and wondered if Charity would want to go along.

And be the third party on the perpetual honeymoon? Charity thought. *No thanks.* Her parents had been married thirty-three years, and they still reminded her of a courting couple when they were able to find some time together away from hectic work schedules and ringing telephones. She would only be an infringement on their hard-earned time alone.

Steven was seeing a nice girl and it was beginning to look serious. Charity grinned. *Wishful thinking, Mom.* Steven was always seeing a nice girl—or two, or three—and it was *never* serious.

Could Charity send an autographed copy of one of her books to be auctioned at the Churchwomen's Service League fund-raiser? "The group is making the request despite old Mrs. Pennypacker's objection that parts of your books tend to be naughty," Mrs. Lovejoy wrote. In parentheses, she added, "Don't be offended—Mrs. Pennypacker is still upset that they allowed Rhett Butler to say damn in the movie version of *Gone With the Wind*."

Charity chuckled at the wry wit so characteristic of her mom as she skimmed over the usual closing sentiments. A sudden warm, reassuring awareness of being part of a family that loved unquestioningly and without reservation surged over her as she put the letter back into the envelope. And she was reminded again, conversely, of those buff-colored envelopes in Lance's mail reminding him of his disenfranchisement from his son's life.

Did he miss his wife, too? she wondered, pressing her head against the back of the sofa and closing her eyes. She opened them momentarily when O.J. landed in her lap unexpectedly, and then closed them again as she absently massaged the cat's ears. "He's a nice person, O.J.," she said softly. "He doesn't deserve such a bum break."

She tried to recall everything she'd read about Charlie in *The Cost of Being a Cop*. She remembered that she had been touched by the story, but the details eluded her. Opening one eye, she confirmed that her copy of Lance's book was still on the coffee table where she'd left it after asking him to autograph it, and she reached out and picked it up.

Before opening it, she shifted into a more comfortable reading position, drawing her legs underneath her and cozying against the corner of the sofa more snugly. O.J. ceased his purring and gave a halfhearted mew of protest at being jiggled before resettling in the crook of her knees and slipping back into an ecstatic stupor as Charity stroked the underside of his chin. His purr had become a snore when Charity ceased the stroking and picked up the book again.

She paused before opening it, suddenly reluctant to confront the story. Knowing Lance had been writing about his own experiences and feelings made it seem as intrusive as reading a diary.

It took several minutes to find the passage she was looking for, and still she hesitated before allowing herself to read it. And when she did, she felt as though her heart had leapt into her throat and become lodged there.

He listened to her saying she was leaving and tried to be sad, but he couldn't feel anything. His emotions were paralyzed. He wasn't even shocked. He realized the inevitability of it, recognized that they had been heading for this final showdown. He wanted to say he was sorry but understood it was too late for apologies.

He knew she was moving out that day, but it was still a shock to find her side of the closet empty, and discover there was only one toothbrush and his shaving gear left in the bathroom. How many times had he complained about the way her makeup and facial cleansers hogged the vanity?

He wondered why he couldn't feel sadness instead of this consuming emptiness. Weeks passed and he waited for the sadness. He had the feeling it was stalking him, waiting for an unguarded moment to pounce on him. Then, just when he'd thought it would never catch up with him, he received official notification that she had started divorce proceedings. Stoically he read the affidavit, folded it, put it away as though it were a product warranty on an appliance. He went to the weight bench and started working out, physically pushing himself to the limit. And when he finally added so much weight on the bar that he couldn't lift it, while he strained against the impossible, the grief descended over him with abject cruelty.

He shouted no like a madman, and then surrendered to the sobs he could no longer hold back. They racked his big body, and he wondered if he would die from the convulsions of them, if his heart would rip apart from the strain of them. Eventually they subsided, though, and he realized his heart was still intact, still performing the function of delivering blood to his body and oxygen to his brain. Yet he didn't feel alive anymore. Part of him had died with the marriage, and he didn't know if that part of him would ever be resurrected.

A week later she telephoned. "The attorneys wanted to contact you, but I said I had to talk to you personally," she said. "There's a problem with the divorce. We'll have to postpone it a few months. I'm pregnant."

The news hit him like a billy club in his guts. "Now don't get the wrong idea, Charlie, I still want the divorce..."

But sure that she would change her mind, he impulsively hopped a plane to the midwest to do in person what he'd been unable to do over the phone. It was futile. She wouldn't yield, not an inch, not even after he'd offered to give up all the off-duty jobs and promised to spend every off-duty hour as a full-time family man. In desperation he even said he'd leave the force, but that made no difference, either.

"You made your choice every day for over three years," she said. "Over a thousand times. Give it up. It's over."

On the way home he tried to convince himself that she was right. It was over between them. It was too late, even if she'd been willing to give it one more try.

His plane was late getting into Tampa, and as he entered the terminal, his first thought was that he was going to have to rush to get home and into uniform in time to make his next shift.

He went back to the midwest when his son was born. It was against hospital policy for anyone except mothers to hold the infants, but Mary explained the situation to the head nurse, who called the doctor who called whoever had the authority to bend policy, and Charlie, in a surgical scrub suit, was allowed to hold his son in his arms. What astounded him most was how tiny the infant was, how defenseless. It gripped his finger in its tiny hand and held it as though it knew it was his father holding him.

Now, he thought. Now Mary would have to understand that they had to be together, the three of them. But before he could say it, she said, "There's something I have to tell you." He knew her well enough to tell just from the way she had said it that whatever she had to say was bad news.

"I've met a man," she said. "We're going to get married as soon as . . . a few weeks after the divorce becomes final."

Ironically, she was marrying an associate at the law firm handling the divorce. He thought nothing could be worse, but in the next instant he was to learn that something could. Something could be much, much worse.

"He wants to adopt the baby," she said. "It'll be easier on the child if he grows up with the same name as his mother."

Charlie felt as though she'd plunged a knife into his chest. He said no at first, but eventually he relented in the face of the facts. It *would* be easier for the kid to have the same name as his parents. He had to think about the child. So, after being assured he would be able to visit his son and that the boy would be told about his parentage when he was old enough to understand, he signed the papers entrusting his son to another man. Though he used the pen the lawyer handed him, he felt like he was signing in blood instead of ink, and the message was clear to him: he'd had to choose between being a cop and being a husband and father. Like she'd said, he'd made the choice a thousand times, ignoring Mary's pleas to spend more time with her, to give up the extra jobs, to quit taking his cases home with him. He could have been a family man now, with a good woman and a beautiful child. Instead, he was a cop.

The fact that he was a damned good cop was no consolation at all.

"No wonder he doesn't believe in happily ever after," Charity said aloud, burrowing her fingers in O.J.'s thick fur. O.J.'s only response was a protracted snore. Charity plumped a throw pillow under her head and laid her head against it wearily. The lazy afternoon spent in the sunshine caught up with her, making her drowsy. She allowed herself a few minutes of indulgent relaxation and then, carefully sliding O.J. from her legs onto the couch, got up to take a shower before the evening news.

Letting warm soapy water rinse away the grime of outdoor recreation was easy, but Charity found ridding herself of the thoughts of Lance and his failed marriage and estranged son wasn't nearly so simple. She kept seeing the resolute set of Lance's jaw as he held the buff envelope, hearing the bitterness and guilt in his voice as he talked about his son.

Tears slid over her cheeks and blended with the shower water flowing into the drain. It wasn't unusual for Charity to empathize with people she cared about. Maybe it was an inevitable side effect of having been raised in the home of a compassionate and people-oriented minister, or maybe her compassionate nature was a gift of heredity. But more than one of Charity's friends had teased her about getting her book ideas by listening to the problems of all her friends. Still, the intensity of her feelings about Lance's situation was extreme, even for her. She was reacting on so many planes and psychological levels that she couldn't isolate her emotions: sympathy, empathy, pity, remorse, compassion, even a trace of something that felt like jealousy over the love Lance had shared with his ex-wife before their divorce.

The jealousy threw her. Was she so taken by him that she could be jealous of a woman who shared his life six years ago? A woman who was irreversibly out of his life?

A woman who hurt him badly, walked out of his life and then replaced him the way she'd replace a shoe that was out of style, she thought bitterly. *A woman who turned him inside out by giving his son to another man.*

She gripped the handle to turn off the shower, wishing she could turn off her vindictiveness as well. She wasn't usually catty and judgmental. If Katy had truly believed her marriage to Lance was unsalvageable, what was so wrong with her getting on with her life, finding another man and doing everything in her power to give her child a stable, loving home life?

She hurt Lance, Charity thought frantically. *She left him bitter and frustrated and guilty, and now he doesn't believe in love anymore, and everyone needs to believe in love, especially Lance.*

She was bending over, toweling her legs, and she jerked upright to attention. Why "especially Lance"?

Stark naked, Charity stood in the small bathroom and pondered the question to which there must be at least a dozen answers. Lance was a nice person, for starters, and nice people should be happy; he certainly wasn't going to be happy as long as he was carrying around that chip of bitterness on his shoulder. And he was sensitive. Sensitive people weren't supposed to be cynical; it went against their grain and made them miserable.

Catching sight of herself in the mirror above the vanity, Charity stared at the naked woman with the wet hair and freshly scrubbed face, feeling suddenly vulnerable and exposed, not because of her nakedness but because she was alone with the one person from whom she couldn't hide her innermost feelings. Her eyes narrowed shrewdly at the reflection of her own face and she challenged aloud, "Why don't you just admit that you're falling in love with him?"

Unable to phrase even a token denial, the naked woman with the wet hair and freshly scrubbed face just stared back at her.

Chapter Nine

Charity studied the hole in the top of her satin scuff and decided two things: the first was that she was going to have to buy a new pair of slippers the next time she was at the mall; the second was that she couldn't possibly be falling in love with Lance Palmer.

She could live with the fact that Lance Palmer was an attractive, virile man and there was a hefty measure of sexual chemistry at work between them when they were together. She could also live with the fact that Lance was a nice person and she enjoyed his company. But falling in love? No matter how sympathetic she was to the extreme circumstance that had driven him to hard-core cynicism, she couldn't even consider falling in love with a confirmed bachelor who had lost his faith in love and wore his resolve not to make commitments like a badge of honor.

Besides, falling in love didn't feel like this. She ought to know—wasn't she an expert in romance? She wrote stories that set hearts pounding and lips sighing. She wouldn't be lying on the sofa thinking that she needed a new pair of house slippers in one breath and wondering if she could be in love in the next if she really was in love. She would *know*.

Granted, she had never personally been in love. She had been infatuated and in "like" and occasionally briefly in "lust," but she'd never met just the right person with whom to fall in love.

Love was not something she could take lightly. To Charity Lovejoy, love was the dream, the ultimate sharing of oneself. Love was commitment and all that commitment entailed; it was trust and respect and a home and, ultimately, children. It was facing life together and growing old together and needing each other.

And love—true love—was not one-sided. It was mutual. As the old song went, it takes two to tango, and Lance Palmer made a point of not hearing the music. Therefore the entire idea of being in love with him was insane. Except that, in point of fact, she was lying on the sofa staring at the hole in her slipper and wondering if she was, against all reason and logic and possibility, falling in love with Lance Palmer, and reaching the impossible conclusion that she didn't know, which meant that she might be.

A weary, languid sigh eased its way through her lips. Wasn't this a hoot? If her fans could see her now, stretched out on the sofa with a burly orange cat asleep on her midriff and a hole in her slipper, if they could read the uncertainty in her mind, she'd probably never sell another book. Cookbook authors knew how to cook. Authors of fitness manuals were physically fit. It just carried over that romance authors were supposed to know when they were in love, and that they never, *ever* fell in love with the wrong person.

Of course, she reasoned, romance authors were not supposed to sleep alone, either, or even with beat-up old tomcats, but that was exactly what Charity was about to do. The television news was over, and it had been a long day. A very long day.

"Door's open, Charity. Come on in."

Tilly, at least, met her as she opened the door. She reached down to give the dog a hasty obligatory pat before following the sound of Lance's voice into the kitchen. He was on the phone, and looked at her from over the receiver. He said, "Why don't you tell her yourself, Tony? She just walked in. Yeah. Here she is."

Tony was as ebullient as ever. "Hey, sweetheart. How does it feel to be on the brink of big-time success?"

"You liked it?" Charity asked, a wide smile brightening her face. She and Lance had mailed him the synopsis and first three chapters of *The Carlotta Chronicles* the preceding week.

"Like it? Sweetheart, I loved it. It's just what we were hoping for. The only question is how soon and how much."

"Why don't you try to work up some enthusiasm for it before you take it to the publisher?" Charity said wryly.

"I don't have to work up enthusiasm on this one, babe. We've got a winner here. Maybe even movie rights. I was just telling Lance that I want you two to be thinking in terms of a sequel as you close this one up. I'm going to push for a two-book contract."

"That's great," she said, but her initial relief and delight that Tony had liked the book faded with the mention of a sequel. She and Lance had not discussed working together beyond the completion of *The Carlotta Chronicles* except in the vaguest terms. She didn't know how Lance would feel about a contractual commitment that would link them professionally for at least another year. Worse, she didn't know how she felt about it.

Tony launched into a pep talk about keeping up the good work, but Charity lost track of what he was saying. "I'll put Lance back on," she said and, handing Lance the receiver, crossed the room to pour herself a cup of coffee.

Cupping the mug of hot coffee in her hands, she blew on the steaming coffee to cool it slightly and took a cautious sip as she peered through the window at the sandy landscape that had become as familiar to her as the view from the front window of her own home.

Lance walked up behind her after he'd hung up the phone. Putting his hands on her shoulders, he massaged her neck with his thumbs. "Good morning."

Charity closed her eyes and concentrated on not letting her shoulders relax against the inviting warmth of his chest. "Good morning."

"Tony thinks it'll fly."

"He was genuinely enthused, wasn't he?"

Lance chuckled. "He'd already wound down by the time he talked to you. You should have heard him when he first got started."

"It's always nice to start out a day with good news."

He nudged the hair off her neck with his nose and kissed her nape. "This is nicer."

Charity lost the battle of resistance. As her shoulders melded against his chest, she asked, "Did he mention a sequel to you?"

"How about that?" Lance said. "A two-book contract. It shouldn't be too hard to adapt the ending to set up a sequel. We didn't give it a pat happily-ever-after anyway."

"No," Charity agreed absently. "We didn't." Lance had made it crystal clear what he thought of happily-ever-after endings—in books or in real life—from the very beginning of their collaboration. And though he kissed her with a tenderness that told her he cared about her, and though he touched her with a gentleness that belied his weight lifter's strength, he never put labels on the feelings he had for her. He told her she was sweet or that being with her was nice, but he never said, "You're special to me," or, "I care about you."

He kissed her, he hugged her, he said the sweet, flattering things men say to women, but he never committed himself to feelings, never intimated that he wanted their relationship, if he considered it that, to go beyond what it was.

When she was trying to be particularly objective and analytical, Charity wondered if he thought of her as anything beyond a writing partner who happened to be female and, therefore, offered the advantage of being kissable and huggable. But when they were together and he was teasing her about something or smiling at her, she was neither objective nor analytical, and she sensed intuitively that she was more to him than just a convenient squeeze. When he was touching her, she lost the faculties of objectivity or analysis. When he was touching her, it was enough that he was special to her.

She had long since quit wondering if she were falling in love with him, and started worrying about how soon the differences in their attitudes toward love and commitment were going to launch them onto an inevitable emotional collision course. She didn't understand his attitude or what she perceived as the vagaries of the male mind. He must know as well as she that what was going on between them could not simply continue. It would intensify or it would fizzle, and either one could affect their professional relationship in a disastrous way. Yet he was ready to commit himself to working with her on a long-term basis without the slightest hesitation.

"Charity?"

She cocked her head so she could see his face.

"You seem subdued," he said. "Aren't you glad that Tony liked *The Carlotta Chronicles*?"

Charity raised the coffee mug to her lips and took a leisurely sip before answering. "Yes. Of course I am." She forced a smile. "I guess it takes a while for good news to sink in."

He slipped his arms around her waist and hugged her slightly. "Why don't we celebrate?"

"Celebrate?"

Chuckling, he said, "A little slow this morning, aren't you? Yes, celebrate. You know, go out and pop a champagne cork, cut loose, have some fun."

"I..."

"Eddie called yesterday and asked if I wanted to meet him tonight for some sort of celebration. He was being very mysterious about it. Why don't I call and see if he wants to get a date and we can make it a foursome?"

"Tonight?"

He kissed the top of her head and laughed. "Drink your coffee, fuzzy head. Yes. Tonight. Unless you have something else planned. You don't, do you?"

Half of a foursome was a twosome. He was asking her on a *date*! Suddenly alert, she quipped, "Actually, I did." She sighed wistfully. "But I guess I'll just have to call Tom Selleck and reschedule. Is it nine o'clock in Hawaii yet?''

"The caffeine in that coffee must be working," Lance said dryly. "If we're on for tonight, I'll call Eddie."

"Why don't you call Eddie?" she said.

"Eddie wants to know if you have a sister," Lance said later, covering the mouthpiece of the telephone receiver. Before she could reply, he said, "Just a minute. What's that? Oh. He says preferably a twin sister or one who looks a lot like you."

"Tell him he's full of baloney," Charity said.

"Charity says you're full of . . ."

"And I don't have any sisters, twin or otherwise," she said, loud enough for her voice to be picked up through the receiver.

Lance listened to Eddie a moment and then said, "He said it's too bad about your not having a sister, but a distant cousin might do."

"Sorry," she said.

"A neighbor? The woman who does your hair?" Lance relayed the messages.

"Tell him to find his own date. My neighbors are all recluses, and a man cuts my hair."

"Did you hear that?" Lance asked into the phone, and then laughed at Eddie's reply. "He wants to know if you'd mind being shared," he told Charity, and without waiting for a reply, told Eddie, "absolutely not, old pal. You find your own woman. I'm not sharing, no matter what Charity says."

His tone of voice changed. "What's that, Charity? Damn, Eddie, she likes the sharing idea. She's got it all worked out. I get her from the hour to the half-hour, and you get her from the half-hour to the—Charity, for Pete's sake, stop that! She's assaulting me!" He reached up and grabbed the folded dishcloth with which Charity was harmlessly but irritatingly flagellating his head and shoulders. "I've got to teach this little wildcat a lesson, Eddie. We'll meet you at seven."

Whatever Eddie's parting remark was, it drew a conspiratorial chortle of male laughter. Lance hung up the phone and turned his full attention to Charity.

Charity didn't like the look in his eye one bit. It was more predatory than aggressive and it gave her a weird feeling in the pit of her stomach that was more excitement than fear.

"Wanna play rough, huh? Wanna get physical?"

"Lance," she said, trying rather unsuccessfully to sound authoritative. "I was only playing, Lance. You were teasing me."

"Only playing, huh?" he said, snapping the dishcloth between his hands. "Just a game?"

Charity hadn't been raised with an older brother without learning a few combat techniques—including the art of diversion and escape. "What's wrong, Palmer, can't take it?" she said, and while he was still reacting to the unexpected allegation, dashed past him and darted into the bathroom, locking the door behind her.

A blow that could have come only from Lance's fist vibrated the door. "Charity," he said, "Charity, open this door immediately."

She bit her lip to keep from laughing at the indignant outrage in his raised voice. A long silence ensued.

"Charity, I mean it. Open the door."

Still that absolute silence from behind the door. Lance heaved a heavy, exasperated sigh. Damned women never played fair! "Charity. Open the door. I was only teasing."

The silence stretched. And stretched. Lance impatiently shifted his weight from one foot to the other and glowered at the door while he zealously fought the urge to kick it in. Finally he dug the knife-cum-clippers from his pocket and started picking the lock. It was one of those locks designed to be opened easily with a screwdriver or other flat, thin blade. He paused with his hand on the knob. "Charity, I've picked the lock. If there's any reason you don't want me to come in there, you'd better say so." For good measure, he added firmly, "Immediately."

Dead silence. He turned the knob. Charity was standing in front of the mirror, toying with her hair. After a few seconds she turned to face him, as though his being there were a complete surprise. "Oh, hi, Lance. I didn't realize you were there."

He'd never been more tempted to strangle someone in his life. "Enjoying yourself?" he asked dryly.

"Actually, no," she said, turning her attention back to the mirror and frowning at her reflection. She reached up to touch a rebellious curl. "This damned cowlick in the front of my hair keeps messing up the line of the style."

Maybe strangling was a bit severe, Lance decided. Maybe he'd settle for just maiming her a little. "Looks okay to me," he said.

She sighed an exasperated sigh. "Men. No sense of style at all. Except for Jacques, of course. My hair stylist. This cowlick drives him absolutely to the brink of despair."

"Only a wimp would be driven to the brink of despair over a cowlick."

"Jacques is not a wimp," she said, as though the idea was absurd. "Jacques is...sensitive. He's an artist with hair."

Lance was suddenly struck by the image of Jacques—*sensitive* Jacques—running his hands through Charity's hair, feeling its silky softness with his fingertips. Strangling would *not* be too severe for Jacques the *artiste*. A muscle flexed in his cheek as he clenched his jaw tightly. His nostrils flared as he heaved a deep breath in his fight for control of his raging emotions. "Has anyone ever told you that you are the most exasperating woman on this earth?"

Charity's eyebrows flew up. "Goodness, no. Steven used to get irritated at me, which is par for the course with a little sister, and during my teen years I managed to surprise my father into speechlessness on occasion, which, with an articulate minister, is no mild achievement. But me—the most exasperating woman on earth?"

Shaking her head, she repeated the phrase. "The most exasperating woman on earth! Honestly! I'm just an easygoing, mild-mannered, old-fashioned girl."

Maiming wouldn't do. It wouldn't do at all. No, maiming was out of the question. Cupping her elbow in his hand, he said, "An *exasperating*, easygoing, mild-mannered, old-fashioned girl."

The look in his eyes softened as he put his fingers under her chin to tilt her face toward his. "As an easygoing, all-American male..."

"Yes?" she asked expectantly.

His hand slid around her shoulders. "I just got an old-fashioned urge," he said, and, closing his arm around her, drawing her near, he kissed her in a most old-fashioned, elemental way that left her breathless and clinging to him for support.

"Lance," she said, and when he nuzzled the top of her head with his chin and murmured an indistinct, "Mmm?" she wanted to ask him a dozen urgent, pressing questions. She wanted to ask him what she meant to him, how important she was to him, if her feelings for him could ever put enough salve on his old emotional wounds to enable him to believe in love again. She wanted, while she was folded in his arms, to say she loved him in a way she'd dreamed of loving a man and hear him say he loved her, too. But courage failed her, and self-preservation made her say, mischievously, "I think Eddie should take the hour to the half-hour, and you should take the half-hour to the hour."

His hold on her tightened perceivably, almost threateningly in a way. "You heard what I told Eddie. He can find his own woman. I'm not sharing."

As he lowered his lips over hers again, Charity took solace in the fact that, although she'd asked none of the questions, she'd gotten an answer of sorts, and it wasn't exactly discouraging. For an evening, at least, she was going to be Lance's woman exclusively. And the word partner hadn't come up at all.

Charity didn't feel guilty about insisting on leaving early so she could shower and dress for the evening. "Are you sure you don't want me to meet you in Tampa?" she asked. In order for them to ride in the same car, Lance was going to have to drive south to Lakeland to pick her up, west to Tampa, then south again to take her home before heading back to Aripeka.

"I'm sure," Lance said. He'd had his fill of watching her drive off into the darkness while he wondered if she'd make it home safely. Tonight he didn't want to have to settle for a cursory good-night kiss as she climbed into her car. Tonight he would do it by the rules—picking her up, opening the car doors for her, pulling out her chair at dinner. And when it came time for good-night kisses, he planned to do something about those old-fashioned urges she aroused in him.

Eddie's date, Marissa, was a striking young woman with a dynamite figure and a pleasant face framed by a cap of kinky brown hair. She was friendly, if a little reserved, until Eddie made the introductions. "You're not Charity Lovejoy the writer, are you?" she asked, awed by the possibility.

Charity answered with a simple, "Yes, I am."

"Just wait until the girls in the office hear about this," Marissa said. "Debbie, that's my boss, buys all your books and we pass them around the office. I loved the one about the professor and the dancer."

"Lance is a writer, too," Eddie interjected. "You probably heard about his book *The Cost of Being a Cop*."

Marissa shook her head. "I'm sorry. I don't think I've read it."

"It was about cops in Tampa," Eddie said.

Marissa shrugged. "Sorry. I just read romances." She addressed Charity. "Have you ever considered writing a historical? I love books about pirates."

A peculiar sound issued from Lance's throat. He was watching Charity intently, and raised his eyebrows almost imperceptibly when she glanced at him. "Actually," she said, "Lance and I are working on a book together. It's a romantic suspense."

"No pirates," Lance said. "We tried, but we couldn't work them into the story." He struggled to keep a straight face as Charity thrust her elbow into his ribs under the table.

"Too bad," Marissa said.

The waiter arrived with the wine they'd ordered and filled their glasses.

"What are we celebrating, Eddie?" Lance said. "You were very mysterious about it."

Eddie appeared self-conscious suddenly, and a flush crawled up his neck and over his cheeks. "It's no big deal. I just made a decision this week, and I wanted you to know about it."

"Well, do we have to pull it out of you like teeth? Quit playing a man of mystery and tell us what this is all about," Lance nagged in a friendly way.

"It sounds kind of lame when I say it, and maybe it's a little premature to celebrate, but I've—" Eddie took a deep breath and announced, "I've decided to go back. I'm going to be a cop again."

A silence fell over the table. Finally, Marissa said, "I didn't know you'd ever been a cop."

Eddie slid his forefinger over the rim of his wine glass and stared at the bubbles floating from the bottom of the glass to the surface of the wine. "It seems like a long, long time ago."

"Well, what are we waiting for? Let's drink to your success at becoming a cop," Lance said, raising his glass. The others followed suit and they clinked glasses and drank the toast.

An awkward silence followed, during which they all sipped at their wine. Finally, Lance asked, "Are you going back with the Tampa P.D.?"

Eddie shook his head and exhaled a sigh. "No. It's too late for that. I need a fresh start, a new location. I'm putting together a packet and querying a dozen or so departments across the country." Directing a crooked grin in Lance's direction, he said, "I was hoping since we'd been partners, and you're a hotshot writer now, you might come up with a letter of recommendation. You know, one of those to-whom-it-may-concern things."

"You got it, buddy," Lance said.

"Didn't you say you two had something to celebrate, too?" Eddie asked.

Lance said, "You know Charity and I have been working on a book... Well, last week we sent a partial of the manuscript—that's a brief description of the book and the first three chapters—to our agent, and he's very optimistic. He told us to be thinking in terms of a sequel."

"You're going to be famous!" Marissa exclaimed. "I'm going to buy your book and have you autograph it and then I'll be able to say I knew you when."

Laughing, Charity said, "I don't know about famous. Right now we're just at the optimistic stage. In this business, though, you don't believe anything until you see it in writing."

"You're already famous," Marissa said. "And I think we should drink another toast to the success of your new book."

"Hear, hear," Eddie said, raising his glass.

"You're not going to get an argument from either of us," Lance said, putting his hand over Charity's and smiling at her warmly.

After drinking the toast, Charity said, "Well, Marissa. What about you—there must be something you can celebrate tonight, too."

"I can't think of anything," Marissa said.

"What about the new car you're going to buy from me this week?" Eddie asked.

"You know I haven't quite made up my mind on that," Marissa said.

"Then let's drink to your making up your mind," Eddie said.

"You certainly have some unusual sales techniques," Marissa said.

"You mean Eddie brought you here to try to sell you a car?" Lance asked incredulously.

"Not true!" Eddie protested. "She's a foxy-looking lady. Just because she's shopping for a car..." His voice trailed off when he discovered that both women were laughing and there was a look of genuine amusement on Lance's face.

"Admit it," Lance said. "We're on to you. Why don't we just drink to happy things happening to Marissa."

"To happy things," Eddie said, relieved, and Charity admired anew Lance's uncanny ability to take the strain out of awkward situations.

With the toasts out of the way, the meal passed pleasantly enough. Dinner conversation was light, and they laughed a lot at inconsequential witticisms and things that were funny only because they were four people intent on having a good time. Charity thoroughly enjoyed herself. She liked Eddie and Marissa, and Lance was attentive and quietly possessive all evening, touching her hand from time to time, winking at her when he chanced to catch her looking at him, whispering little asides into her ear when the conversation got especially lively. While it was officially their first date, it didn't seem like a first date at all because they knew each other so well. It was, she thought, with a stab of longing, as though they'd been going together for a long time, as though they were very committed to one another.

After much debate they decided to take in the nine o'clock showing of a new movie. While the men took care of the check, Charity and Marissa went to the ladies' room to freshen their makeup. "I'm glad I came tonight," Marissa said. "I wasn't sure whether I should or not. I don't know Eddie very well, so I almost said no."

"I'm glad you took the chance. And from the way Eddie's eyeballing you, it's a safe bet he is, too," Charity said.

"Do you think so?" Marissa asked. "I thought maybe I was imagining it. Wishful thinking, or something. I mean, just meeting him at the car lot, I thought Eddie was a little bit flaky, but he's really a neat guy."

"I'm glad things are working out for you," Charity said.

"What's the story on you and Lance?" she said. "Are you engaged or living together or what?"

"Or what," Charity said wryly, thinking bitterly that the question appropriately summed up all the ambiguities of their relationship. "We've been working together, and we've gotten kind of close."

"He's a hunk," Marissa said.

"He lifts weights," Charity replied absently, remembering that just weeks earlier she'd thought him too brawny.

The men had finished with the bill and were waiting for Charity and Marissa in the foyer. Eddie looked at his watch. "I've never figured out what women do in bathrooms that take them so long."

"Woman things," Lance said. "It's a fact of nature."

"So how's it progressing with you and Charity? You two seem cozy enough."

"We're getting there," Lance said.

"Is it serious, or what?"

"Define serious."

"Serious."

"She's fun to work with."

"She's damned sexy, too."

Lance grinned. "Yeah. She kisses good, too."

Eddie grinned back. "That wasn't the question."

Their conversation was left dangling, unfinished, as the women approached, and Eddie said, "You ladies ready to go?"

The movie was zany and entertaining, and they were all in a jovial mood as they stood in the parking lot exchanging the usual pleasantries before breaking into their separate cars. Charity gave Eddie a hug and wished him luck with the resumption of his law-enforcement career and promised to send Marissa an autographed copy of her latest book; Lance shook hands with Marissa and slapped Eddie on the back and promised he'd be in touch with him about the letter of recommendation. They all agreed it had been a wonderful evening and they should do it again soon.

In the relative silence of Lance's car, Charity thought of the conversation with Marissa. ... *Engaged, or living together or what?* Charity pressed her temple against the cool glass and sighed softly in the darkness.

Lance heard the sigh and asked, "Tired?"

"A little."

"It's almost midnight."

Charity straightened in the seat and twisted her head to look at Lance as she spoke to him. "I should have met you in Tampa. It's going to be after two by the time you get back to Aripeka."

"I would have worried about you getting home safely."

They were quiet for a long while. Then Charity said, "Will Eddie be able to find a job as a cop?"

"He should. A lot of departments are crying for experienced officers. He left Tampa P.D. under a cloud, but he left voluntarily. His file is clean. He'll probably end up weighing several offers against each other, seeing which department offers him the best deal, and trying to decide where he wants to live."

"I hope so. As badly as this country needs good cops, it's a shame for a good cop to be selling cars."

Wrapping his hand around Charity's, Lance looked over at her and smiled. "I agree."

When they reached her apartment, Charity suddenly was loath for the evening to end. They had been so relaxed, had so much fun, seemed so *together.* Even Marissa had perceived their closeness.

Lance put his arm across her back and rested his hand on her waist, and she allowed herself to melt into the strength of his body as they walked. He didn't ask to come inside, and she didn't invite him; he merely followed her through the door, and it never occurred to her to protest. "I could make coffee if you like," she said. "To keep you awake on the rest of the drive."

Lance nodded and trailed after her to the kitchen where she set up the percolator and plugged it in. Ordinarily she did not invite men into her apartment after a date, and she suddenly realized that she hadn't the faintest notion what to say to Lance. The comfortable rapport that had been in play between them all evening had evaporated as they walked through the door. His partner would have known what to say; his date didn't.

Very aware of how close he was to her in the small kitchen as he leaned against the counter with his arms crossed over his chest watching her, she focused her attention on the coffeepot as though it required her concentrated stare to start it perking. *Please, Lance,* she thought desperately, *use that talent of yours for soothing over awkward situations to bail us out of this one.*

It was not a magical phrase he came up with this time but a magical touch. His hands lighted on her shoulders and slid down her arms, stopping just above her elbows. He stepped very near her, and she instinctively leaned back, letting her body meld against his. His hands moved forward over her waist until his arms were around her, trapping her own arms against her body. And then, with the gentlest of nudges, he coaxed her into turning around. Their eyes met briefly in a poignant, explicit communication before Lance raised one hand to trace the line of her cheek with his fingertips and then cup her chin as he lowered his lips over her cheek and down her jaw to the enticing velvet skin of her neck.

"You are so sweet," he whispered breathlessly. "So incredibly sweet. I need you, Charity."

There was no time for her to reply before his mouth pressed over hers again and he was teasing her bottom lip with his tongue, urging, seducing her teeth apart so he could probe the soft, private recesses of her mouth. Charity's hands roved over the hard, thick muscles of his back and pressed into his flesh, clinging to him as a hot, pungent need throbbed through her. She felt Lance's hands on her, his strong, gentle fingers caressing and arousing her.

She gasped as his mouth drew away from hers and traveled down to the pulse point of her neck and tasted the salty sweetness of her skin. His hand pressed over her breast through her blouse and his thumb swept over the nipple pressing tautly against the lace of her bra. The hardness of his body pressing intimately against hers left no doubt of the truth of the plea that rasped through his throat as he began working at the button on her blouse: "I want you."

His fingers met the flesh above her bra and then pushed their way inside the delicate lace. The red-hot heat of desire licked around Charity consumingly at his touch. "Love me," she said urgently. "Oh, Lance, love me."

She was not immediately cognizant of the fact that he was withdrawing from her. It wasn't until he reached behind his back to cover her hands with his own and then guide them from around his waist and stepped away from her, turning his back to her, that she realized something was terribly, terribly wrong.

The dejected set of his broad shoulders was starkly revealing, and she extended her arm to touch the sinews crisscrossing those drooping shoulders with trembling fingers. She said his name, uttering it as a question, but he appeared not to hear her, just as he showed no indication that he was aware of her touch. She swallowed to moisten her dry mouth. Her voice still sounded stringy and thin. "Lance, what's wrong?"

"Why did you say that?" he asked. "Why in the hell did you have to say it?" His misery was so real it was almost palpable.

Charity could not think; rational thought was not within her capabilities. She could only react, and her words came without thought, but they were true words, unguarded by the defenses that might have sprung into play if the situation were not so emotional. "I said what I was feeling," she said. "I want you to love me." Her hand crept from his shoulder blade to cup the round cap of his shoulder and squeeze it.

"You're asking too much. Damn it, Charity, you're asking for too much."

"I haven't asked for anything except what you offered," she said softly. "You said you needed me."

He spun around and thrust his face near hers. "Haven't you? If you'd said, 'I need you,' or 'I want you,' or 'Be with me,' I could have said, 'I need you,' or 'I want you,' or 'I'll stay with you.' But you had to bring love into it, and we both know what love means to you."

Turning, he put his hands on the edge of the counter to brace himself as he leaned against it. Charity was left to contemplate the way the cord of muscles on his back tensed under the fabric of his shirt. Her pulse, which had been racing with desire just seconds earlier, hammered now with frustration.

"You can't separate the two," she said. "The way I feel—the way you make me feel—I feel that way because I love you."

After a strained silence, Lance raised his fist and brought it crashing down on the countertop, rattling the coffeepot and the pots and pans stored in the cabinet below. "I don't want to hurt you," he said.

"Then hold me," she said, barely touching his back. Gratefully, oh, so gratefully, she stepped into the circle of his arms and burrowed her face against his chest when he turned to embrace her.

"I want you," he whispered, threading his fingers through her hair, pressing her face closer to his heart. "I want to be with you."

"To be with me," she said, letting out a ragged breath. "Not to make love."

"I would love being with you, but I won't pretend to love you in the way you mean. I won't lie to you or make promises I can't keep."

Blinking back the tears burning her eyes, Charity sucked in a fortifying breath and pulled herself away from him, brushing his arms from around her. All the confusion of the past weeks seemed to be swooping over her, dulling her brain. Shock, incredulity tinged her voice. "What do I mean to you?" And then, "What do you think of when you kiss me?"

He lifted a lock of hair off her shoulder and rubbed it between his thumb and forefinger. "Kissing's not about thinking, Charity, it's about feeling. When I'm kissing you, I feel the way a man is supposed to feel when he kisses a woman. I like the way you fit in my arms and the way your body fits next to mine."

His hand fell to her neck; his fingers warmed the sensitive skin there. "When I'm kissing you, I never want to stop. I just want to keep right on holding you until I absorb you and you're part of me."

How very poignant, Charity thought, her breath quickening involuntarily in response to the sensuality of the blunt statement. *How poignantly he describes desire without mentioning love.* Averting her eyes from his, she happened to catch sight of the coffeepot. "The coffee's ready," she said. "I'll pour you a cup."

His forefinger trailed down from her neck, traced the line of her collarbone, stopping only when it encountered the bodice of her dress. "Charity?" She tilted her head to look up at him, her eyes wide open and a little too bright. "I want you," he said, his voice low and artlessly seductive.

"You want to have sex with me," she said dully.

His eyes narrowed. "Is that an accusation?"

Without answering, she walked to the cupboard where the cups were stored and took out one of the ironstone mugs she'd bought especially for Lance's use because of its weight and large handle. It made a dull thunk when she set it on the counter next to the coffeepot. Wordlessly, she filled the mug and gave it to Lance, who regarded her over its rim as he dutifully took a sip of the steaming coffee.

"It's possible for a man and woman to enjoy each other's company, even to enjoy sex together without being madly in love," he said. "I would think the emerging mistress of the sensitive, sensuous sex scene would know about that."

"The thing that makes my sex scenes work is that my characters care about each other."

"Don't you think I care about you?"

"Do you?" she said, and realized she'd said it too quickly and with too much urgency.

He put down the mug and pulled Charity into his arms, and stroked her hair. "Of course I care. You're special, you're bright and you're fun to be with. And there's not another woman on earth I'd rather be with at this moment.''

Charity closed her eyes and allowed her forehead to sag against his chest while the words *at this moment* sliced at her heart like a twisting knife blade. Sensing her lack of response to him, the involuntary rigidity of her body as it shrank from his, he circled her upper arms with his hands and pushed her far enough away to see her face. ''For God's sake, what do you want from me, Charity?''

Her eyes locked with his. ''I want to be more than the woman of the moment,'' she said.

A groan of pure frustration rose from his chest and gurgled through his throat, and his arms dropped limply to his side. His mouth hardened into a sinister line and then gave way to a scathing expletive, which he said with gusto and repeated with equal exuberance before saying, ''I should have known better! I should have known better than to get mixed up with a woman who spends her life thinking up romantic fairy tales.''

Disappointment, sadness, rage—Charity couldn't have isolated and identified the soup of emotions roiling inside her. An evening filled with sweet promise had turned into a bitter debacle so swiftly that she was reeling with the shock of transition. Confused, hurting, she turned to the source of her confusion and pain and blinked back tears she refused to shed. ''Drink your coffee,'' she said woodenly. ''It's a long drive to Aripeka.''

For several seconds he just stood and stared at her. Then, touching her arm tentatively, he said her name softly. Charity jerked away from him.

''I can't make forever promises to you,'' he said.

"Please, Lance, just leave. It's late."

His mouth was poised with an argument, but she forestalled him with a shake of her head, thinking that if he insisted on arguing with her she'd crumble under the strain of it. "There's no way either of us could salvage this evening," she told him.

After nodding a grudging acquiescence, he raised his hands as though he might be contemplating touching or hugging her, reconsidered, and strode out of the room. Charity sagged against the counter and buried her face in her hands. She heard the front door open with a squeak and snap closed again, and then the consuming silence of late night crept through the apartment like a noxious fog.

Chapter Ten

The doorbell was ringing when Charity stepped out of the bathroom and it pealed again while she was checking the clock on the bedside table. Nearly one-thirty in the morning. She'd been in the tub almost an hour. The bell screeched again, with an urgency that belied its being an inanimate object.

Charity rummaged through her closet for her full-length satin robe, pulled it on over her knit sleep shirt and jammed her feet into her tattered slippers. The bell sounded twice again before she'd crossed the living room and reached the door. A quick check at the peephole eased the fear that a middle-of-the-night ringing of the bell always arouses and confirmed her assumption that Lance was the source of this untimely and noisy intrusion in her life.

Charity opened the door and glowered at him wordlessly. Lance stared back at her contritely. "I got halfway home and turned around," he said, stepping into the apartment. Charity walked to the furniture grouping in the center of the room and plopped down in an armchair, leaving Lance the chore of closing the door.

"I've been ringing the bell for fifteen minutes," he said, settling into the chair opposite hers.

"I was in the bathtub," she said.

"I would have knocked, but I was afraid I would disturb the neighbors."

"You could have left," she said wryly, kicking off her slippers, drawing her knees up to her chest and wrapping her arms around them.

"I wanted to make sure you were all right."

"I'm a big girl," she said. "I don't crumble in the face of a little sexual tension and an awkward proposition."

The difference between the flippant, steel-cored woman she was trying to be and the person Charity was saddened Lance. She looked small and vulnerable with her face freshly scrubbed and her hair curly from the steamy bath and her pink-polished toenails peeping from beneath the hem of the robe.

It seemed to both of them that the silence would crush them before either of them spoke, and then, suddenly, they were both speaking at once.

"I'm sorry," he began, and stopped in mid-thought when he realized she was saying something.

"I...uh..." She drew in a calming breath. "I had some time to think."

"There's no better place for thinking than a bathtub."

Charity tried to summon a small laugh and failed miserably. "I guess not."

He waited patiently, wishing they could get past all this awkward pussyfooting and he could cuddle her in his arms and tell her how sorry he was to have hurt her, how sorry he was that he couldn't whisper the promises she wanted to hear.

"I didn't handle tonight very well," she said.

"It wasn't your fault—" he began, but she stopped him.

"The truth is, I knew from the very first time we met that you and I are philosophical opposites, and yet I let myself fall in love with you." Shaking her head like a boxer dazed by a punch, she raised her hand in the air as though she might collect the words and draw them back the way she would catch an insect.

Her hand clenched into a fist containing nothing but air. "No. That's wrong. I didn't let myself fall in love. I fought it, actually. I just...I just did, that's all. I knew all along it was crazy and impossible, but I fell in love with you anyway."

"Charity—"

"Don't! Please, Lance, let me finish. This is difficult enough. I sat in the bathtub thinking this through until half my skin shriveled up. Let me put it into words." She took a breath. "There's something between us, a chemistry, that doesn't happen too often, not to me, at least—"

"Not for me, either," he interjected.

She continued undaunted. "Anyway, having you apologizing for something that neither of us...well, it's not going to solve anything, so please, let's not get maudlin about it."

He was getting out of his chair, but she extended her arm like a cop halting traffic. "No," she said. "Please.

I think, in light of the situation, we're better off if we stay in separate chairs."

Lance eased back into his own chair, but the frown that had claimed his mouth spread upward to crease his forehead.

"I've fallen in love with you," Charity continued matter-of-factly, "I can't pretend that I haven't. And you were right when you said I want everything to be the way it is in my books. I want love to be forever."

The tears that had remained bottled up when she was alone in the privacy of her bathroom now traitorously refused to be contained. Except for wiping them off her cheeks with the backs of her hand from time to time, she ignored them.

"I care about you a great deal, Charity," he said, wishing again that she would let him comfort her.

"Please don't," she said. "Don't say sweet things to salve my ego. I know you don't want the same things I want. You've been very open and very honest about your opinion of true love and happily ever after, and it wouldn't be fair of me to try to change you."

Her voice abandoned her temporarily, and in the lapse, her name was the only thing Lance could think of to say. She seemed not to hear him and drew in a ragged breath. "I'm very attracted to you, but I can't just have sex with you." She opened her mouth to speak, but nothing came out but the frailest puff of air so she swallowed and tried again. "It has to be the whole package for me. I don't want to have sex, or to 'be with' you. I want to make love and be made love to."

A sob overwhelmed her, and she buried her face in her hands. Lance got up and went to the kitchen and returned with a glass of water and a paper napkin, which he gave to her with a shrug of his shoulders. "It was the closest thing to tissue I could find."

Charity nodded appreciation and after taking a few sips of water, blotted her cheeks, wiped her eyes and blew her nose. Lance sat down on the floor next to her chair and wrapped his hand around hers. Charity smiled down at him courageously. He drew her hand to his lips and kissed her. "It wouldn't be 'just sex.' I do care about you. Just because I can't promise you forever..."

She pulled her hand away. "I know I'm an anachronism," she said. "I've tried to change, but I've just never been able.... I can't help the way I was raised, believing that the family is sacrosanct and that sex is a part of a special kind of love."

"What about the men you knew before me?" Lance asked. "Did you think it was going to be forever with them?"

He watched with disbelief as the color drained from her face and her features took on the heartsick, mortified expression of a person whose innermost secret has been exposed. Still he wasn't quite convinced, couldn't quite comprehend that what her face was telling him so explicitly was true.

He couldn't believe it, but it was true. "My God," he said, "Great holy cow, Charity!"

The color was back in her face. In fact, there was a red stain spreading over her cheeks. "If you laugh I swear I'll kill you with my bare hands."

Abruptly, Lance stood up and paced back and forth across the room several times, and then, as suddenly as he'd sprung to his feet, he stopped his pacing in midstride. "Let me get this straight," he said, impaling her with shrewdly narrowed eyes. "You, Charity Lovejoy, the emerging mistress of the sensitive, sensuous sex scene, are a virgin."

"It's not a crime," she said indignantly. "And it's certainly not a sin."

"It's certainly a shock," he said. "How do you . . . don't you feel like a hypocrite writing those sizzling love scenes?"

"Stephen King isn't a vampire or a hatchet maniac. Agatha Christie wasn't a murderer."

Quite literally, Lance sank onto the sofa, letting his body sag against the plump cushions. "I'm not sure it's the same thing."

"You said it yourself, Lance. I write romantic fairy tales. Maybe I haven't been with a man, but I know what it's supposed to be like. Maybe in my case I fell in love with the wrong man, but that doesn't keep me from imagining what it would be like to love the right man."

A scowl furrowed Lance's brow. "You talk as though . . . Charity, am I the first man you've ever been in love with?"

"Man, yes. I loved a boy in high school, but we were too young for commitments and we both knew it. I've dated, of course, but never seriously. I've *cared for* people the way you care for me, but love is . . ." She tried to smile at him and he felt his heart breaking for her as he noticed the uncommon brightness of her eyes. ". . . it's different, isn't it? And losing it hurts. You wouldn't be afraid of commitment if you hadn't loved Katy."

Lance stared down at his steepled fingers, remembering the shock of hearing Katy say she was leaving. "I'm sorry, Charity," he said. "I'm so sorry."

"It's not your fault. I'm not sure it's anyone's *fault* when someone falls in love. You were just there—big and virile and fun—and I was there, ready to fall in love and I . . . fell in love. You never lied to me." Her voice had trailed off, but it was stronger when she said, "You didn't try to make me fall in love with you."

She got up. "I didn't pour out the coffee before. I'm going to reheat it so you can have a cup before you leave."

"Charity," he said, after following her into the kitchen.

She looked at him pleadingly. "I think I've already said more than I'm going to be happy about having said tomorrow. If you want to do me a favor, please quit feeling guilty for something that's not your fault and let me deal with my problem my own way. It *is* my problem, you know, not yours."

"What about working together?" he asked.

"We're rather committed, aren't we? For *The Carlotta Chronicles*, at least. We'll just have to be adult about it, and get the job done. There's no reason . . ." She was about to say there's no reason they couldn't be friends, but she knew that would be a lie. She couldn't be his friend, not unless friendship was a part of her love for him. She sighed defeatedly. "Just don't touch me, Lance. That's all I ask. When we're working together, just don't . . ."

He was touching her suddenly. His arms were around her, his body was solid against hers and his lips were pressing tiny, soothing kisses on her temple. "I wish . . ." he said sadly and let the thought dangle unfinished.

Charity choked back a sob and pulled away from him, wondering if he knew how much it hurt her to move those few inches, if he could even conceive how much courage it demanded. He'd always accused her of being a dreamer. Now, if he couldn't love her, he'd at least respect the fact that she was able to look reality in the face and accept it with courage and grace.

The next few minutes passed in a blur. The coffee heated. She poured it. Lance drank it. Then, after dropping a final parting kiss on her cheek and hugging her one last time, he left.

Charity did not walk with him to the door, nor did she cross the room to lock the door after he left. She simply stood in the doorway that connected the kitchen and the living room and stared at it, thinking what a dismal sight a closed door could be. She'd have to remember to use a closed door in a book sometime. A door that separated a person from the rest of the world, that cut one off from other human beings.

O.J. meandered into the room from wherever he'd been holed up or curled up sleeping and brushed back and forth against her legs, managing to nudge his way inside the tail of her robe. She bent down and hoisted the cat up into her arms and stroked his chin and waited for the inevitable motorlike purr. "Come on, O.J. It's the middle of the night. Time for bed."

And so Charity Lovejoy, the emerging mistress of the sensitive, sensuous sex scene, went to the bed she shared with her battered old tomcat and wondered, under the cover of darkness, what was so important about forever, and what would be so wrong about sex between a woman who loved and a man who cared.

Chapter Eleven

Erskine flecked at the adhesive tape with his finger-nail, trying to lift the edge far enough to get a grip on it. "Believe me when I tell you this is going to pain me more than it hurts you," he said. "Do you realize this is the first time I've been able to put ten words together without your interrupting me, bossing me, enlightening me with your cockeyed, upside-down logic?" He appeared not to notice the animal-like noises she was making in her frantic effort to speak as he smiled at her sweetly and gripped the edge of the tape between his thumb and forefinger. "Cheer up, sweetheart, it could be worse. At least you don't have a mustache." With that last consoling thought, he removed the tape with a single, excruciating zip.

"Sounds good," Lance said.

"You don't think he sounds a little too callous?"

"After what she's put him through? No. Besides, there's a certain affectionate tone to the hostility. An underriding sexual tension."

Charity propped her elbow on the desk and rested her forehead on her fist and let out an involuntary sigh. Without thinking, Lance reached out to massage her tense neck muscles with his fingers. "Lance," she said, giving his name a censorial tone.

He withdrew his hand instantly and sighed. "This isn't working."

"No," she agreed. The book, to their credit, was getting written, but Charity and Lance were nervous wrecks, both constantly keyed up, walking barefoot over eggshells to keep from touching each other, to pretend they were unaware of the sexual tension between them.

After a long, strained silence, Lance asked, "What are we going to do?"

A bitter laugh rose from Charity's throat. "Any suggestions?"

"You don't want to hear it," he said caustically.

She looked straight into his eyes. "Try me."

Lance met her even gaze, and thought, *Let's quit pretending that we're not attracted to each other. Let's quit thinking, at all. Let's go into your bedroom and shoo that scruffy cat of yours off the bed and lose ourselves in mindless passion.* But he didn't say anything. He was all too cognizant of her vulnerability. He knew he could seduce her into bed with very little effort. And he knew that he would wind up with as many morning-after regrets and as hefty a case of self-loathing as she would.

She was still looking at him expectantly, her face an open book in which he could read her mind and her feelings. He thought, as he looked at that fresh, fetching face, that if he ever felt capable of loving a woman again, he could turn the world upside down and inside out and not find a woman more worthy of love. A pang of regret pierced through him at the loss of the man he once had been, a man who could trust in happiness and sunny tomorrows.

"Take a chance on me," he said, surprising himself as well as her. He stroked her hair lovingly. "Pack up your nightie and your toothbrush and your jeans and your cat and come stay with me."

"Move in with you?" she asked wonderingly.

"Forever is a long, long time, Charity. It's like infinity. I can't envision it. But I could deal with a week or a month, and who knows what would happen?"

"Maybe I'd become a habit," she said, trying to distance herself from him, trying to ignore the way something in her was undermining her sense of self-preservation and telling her to settle for whatever happiness they could find together and then worry about the consequences when it all fell apart.

"Maybe," he said, with a hint of a smile playing at his lips.

How seductive that smile was, how beautiful his lips were. She could almost feel the way they'd move over her own lips, the way they would nibble at the skin on her neck. "I can't be just your habit!" she said emphatically, lecturing the weak, unthinking part of her character that was saying, *why not?* "Habits are so easily broken, Lance. You'd break me."

There was a sadness in his eyes, a hint of regret she'd never seen there before. "That was my suggestion," he said. "What's yours?"

She thought a long time before answering. "We've thought the chapters through in detail. We know what's going to happen in each one, and we're pretty comfortable with our characters now. Why don't we alternate—you take odds and I'll take evens. We can mail each other a printout of each chapter as we finish it, and make edits on the printed copy. Then we can exchange them again and put the revisions into the computer before we print out a final draft."

"I like my suggestion better."

She closed her eyes. "Do you enjoy goading me?"

"No," he said gravely. "I'm not very proud of myself at the moment."

"Do you think it would work?"

"You taking evens and my taking odds and exchanging chapters?" He considered the idea a moment. "It's worth a try. Right now I'd say it's our best shot at getting this book written without going stark raving mad."

"It might be better if we set a time frame," she said, policing her mind, forcing it to focus only on the job. "Say, a week per chapter. That way we can read each other's chapters and work as much in sequence as possible. If we don't, we're going to have problems with inconsistency. With the two of us doing separate chapters, we're going to have to be careful about consistency anyway. Hopefully by editing each other's work, we'll smooth most of them out."

"What about this chapter?" he said. "Do you want to try to finish it together? We could pick up a quick dinner somewhere and work until it's done."

She shrugged. "There are only a few pages left. I don't mind finishing it up before I start my next chapter."

"Whatever you say," Lance said, acknowledging that she was inviting him to leave. Was it possible to hate love? he wondered as they walked to the living room. Like—like was nice. Like was realistic. Love just gummed up the works. *Why, Charity? Why can't you just settle for a meaningful relationship? Why does it have to be love or nothing with you?*

He stopped in the middle of the living room. It was time for gallantry, the only type of gallantry of which he seemed capable. "About the contract," he said, and she raised an eyebrow, alert, waiting for him to finish the thought. "I don't see how we could pull this book out from underneath Tony. But if you don't feel right about a sequel, I mean about the long-term commitment to work with me . . ." He heaved an exasperated sigh. "What I'm trying to say is that it's good business, but neither of us is going to starve if we decide not to do a sequel. I've still got a good cushion from *Cop*, and you said your romance publisher is breathing down your neck for another book, so if you'd rather not, I'd understand."

He was giving her an out, making it easy for her. Charity recognized the gallantry and was touched by it. "We don't have to make a decision immediately," she said. "It'll be weeks, possibly months before the publisher makes any firm offer. Why don't we see how the alternate-chapter routine works?"

"It's up to you," he said. "Like you said, it'll be weeks before we have to make any decisions."

But it wasn't weeks. With a perverse departure from the way the New York publishing industry usually operates, an offer came much earlier than expected. It was only six days later that Charity returned from having her hair trimmed at the salon to find a notice on her doorknob that a delivery addressed to her had been left at the apartment office. Expecting to collect a set of galleys, which her publisher always sent via express mail, she found herself instead carrying a box of long-stemmed roses back to her apartment. After removing the wide red bow of floral ribbon, she opened the box to find the card. It read, "Offer made on *Carlotta Chronicles*—excellent terms—Tony will call later."

Sinking wearily onto the sofa, she absently stroked O.J. who, after having been shooed away from the roses, had decided to take solace for his hurt pride by curling up in her lap.

Damn! Charity thought. Damn! Damn! Damn! She wasn't going to have several weeks to make a decision. She had to make it immediately. Tony wouldn't let her stall much over a day or two, she was sure. Why in the hell did her personal life have to be linked to her professional life, anyway? How had she allowed herself to get into a position where she had to sacrifice one or the other—and where if she sacrificed the professional opportunity, she'd be hurting someone else's career, too?

How had she let herself fall in love with Lance Palmer?

Tony called around four o'clock. "You're home," he said ebulliently upon hearing her voice. "I take it you got my message."

"I did, and I must say I like your style," she answered. "The roses are beautiful. I take it the offer was good."

"Roses?" he asked.

"Don't be coy, Tony. The very expensive long-stemmed roses with the note that said there's been an offer and you'd call later."

"I'm going to remember the approach, sweetheart, but I didn't send any roses. When I got your answering machine this morning I called Lance and asked him to tell you I'd be calling back after a meeting this afternoon."

"Lance?" she said, trying to reconcile Lance's decidedly unromantic ideology with the decidedly romantic gesture of sending a woman long-stemmed roses.

"The man you're collaborating with," Tony said. "I discussed the terms with him, and he said the ball's in your court now."

With a marked lack of enthusiasm, Charity said, "What was the offer?"

It was, she realized as she listened to Tony detailing the amount of money the publisher was offering and the terms of the contract, an excellent deal. She and Lance would be getting a generous advance for the *Carlotta Chronicles*, an even more generous advance upon approval of an outline of an appropriate sequel and an option on a third book to be negotiated at the time of submission, which meant if sales of *Carlotta* were good, they were free to push for a much higher advance for the third book.

After sucking in a calming breath, she asked tentatively, "Is the offer on *Carlotta* firm? I mean, if we should decide not to do a sequel, can we get the contract for the one book?"

"Jehosephat! Charity? Why in the world would you do a lamebrained, idiotic thing like that?"

Because I'm a lamebrained, lovesick idiot, that's why, thought Charity. But she said, "We...I'm...Lance and I just aren't sure whether a collaboration is going to work indefinitely."

"Jiminy Cricket, are you two still at each other's throats? You sure can't tell it from your work. Aren't you two creative geniuses mature enough to work out your differences?" After a dead silence, he added, "Lance didn't mention any problems with the sequel."

"He told me it was up to me," she said quickly, momentarily resenting the responsibility Lance had piled on her shoulders. "Anyway, Tony, we're not at each other's throats. It's not that. It's . . . personal."

Tony muttered a shocking expletive. "Don't tell me you two have fallen in love."

"One of us has," she said dismally. Since he had a percentage interest in their work, Tony had a right to know about anything extraordinary that was influencing the decisions of his clients.

The scathing expletive skittered through the phone system again. "How bad is the situation? You're finishing *Carlotta*—can't you keep on working, on a strictly professional level? You'd be crazy to blow this."

"Is the offer on *Carlotta* solid?" she asked.

"Yes."

"And the option would cover only books we write together—it wouldn't keep us from pursuing other projects individually?"

"That's right. But Charity, be reasonable. It's a better deal with the sequel. Don't do anything foolish."

"When do you have to get back to the publisher?"

"As soon as possible." He sighed. "Look, it's a little late today anyway, so I'll call you Monday morning. That'll give you the weekend to think it over."

Thinking it was fairer than she deserved, she agreed.

Charity reached into the most remote corner of her top cupboard for one of the cut-crystal wineglasses she kept there and carried it to the table. There, next to the vase of roses and a plate of pasta salad, which had been purchased at a deli, a bottle of white Rhine wine was chilling in an insulated ice bucket. Charity lifted the bottle of wine, blotting its wetness with a linen napkin, and began working at the cork with her plunger-style corkscrew. It surrendered with a respectable popping noise, and she filled the wineglass. "To decisions," she said, toasting the air.

She couldn't remember ever having had a more solitary meal or a more dismal one. By all rights, she should be out somewhere celebrating her new prosperity. She and Lance should be celebrating *their* prosperity together.

Instead, here she was, eating alone, drinking alone, pondering a decision still unmade, trying to choose between what was right for her personally and what was right for her and Lance professionally.

After finishing her salad, she poured herself another glass of wine and carried it, along with the bottle, to the sofa, where she sank against the plump cushions and sighed. She seldom drank more than a second glass of wine, and she was feeling the effects of the second drink—a creeping numbing of the senses that took the sharp edge from her misery—almost immediately.

O.J. approached, mewing for attention, while Charity was filling her glass for the third time. "Don't lecture me," Charity said indignantly. "I'm in love with the wrong man, my best friend is out of town and I'm stuck with a real bummer of a decision. Of all the people in all the world, no one is more entitled to get a little tipsy on celebratory wine than I am tonight."

Uncomprehending, O.J. leapt onto the couch, walked the length of Charity's thigh like a child balancing on a railroad track and, perching precariously on Charity's hip, sniffed at the glass. Charity jerked it out of his reach. "No, no. Cats don't get wine. Wine is for people. Maybe I'll become a wino. Do you think they'd write me up in the romance magazines, O.J.?" She rejected the idea with an unsteady bobbing of her head. "No. Of course not. Supermarket tabloids would be more like it. *Romance Writer, Spurned in Love, Buries her Sorrow in Liquor.* I'll see it when I'm in line at the supermarket buying cat food and cheap wine."

Downing what remained in the glass in a single draft, she plunked the glass on the end table gracelessly and stood up, dumping O.J. from her lap.

"I don't want to be in the supermarket tabloids," she said. "I don't want to become a wino." Suddenly she felt like bawling. A tear was already coursing down her cheek. "I don't want to end up an old maid who eats and drinks alone and talks to cats."

O.J., offended by the abrupt ouster, was nowhere around, but Charity didn't notice. "You know what's the pits?" she asked the silent room. "I'll tell you what's the pits. Being the last twenty-seven-year-old virgin on the face of the earth is the pits."

Chapter Twelve

Charity opened one eye halfway and reached for the telephone, wondering why she'd never before noticed how rude the shrill ring of a telephone could be. "Hello," she said, wincing as a pain shot through her head. Quickly she folded her left arm across her face to shield her eyes from the ridiculously bright sunlight filtering through the bedroom window's blinds. "What's that? Oh, yeah, Mom. I was still asleep. No, don't be silly. It's time I was awake. What time is it anyway?"

"It's ten o'clock," her mother reported. "Charity, are you all right? You sound different."

"I slept too long. I'm just groggy," Charity said, deciding it would not be wise to confide in her mother that she was suffering from the first bona fide hangover in her life. "Are you okay, Mom? And Dad? There's nothing wrong, is there?"

"We're all just fine," Mrs. Lovejoy assured her. "I was just thinking about you and hadn't heard from you since last week, so I wanted to call and say hello. How's your work?''

"It's . . . it's okay," Charity said, but her timing was off. She tried to cover by adding, quickly and too brightly, "We got an offer on the book we're working on. It's a good offer."

"Good," Mrs. Lovejoy said. "That's good news. Congratulations." After a long, pregnant pause, she said, "I don't want to meddle, Charity, but if you've got a problem, you can tell me about it. There's not much I haven't heard before. Maybe I can help."

Suddenly there was nothing Charity wanted more than to tell her mother all about falling in love with Lance and the hopelessness of the relationship. She would have liked, at that moment when she was miserable and feeling very inexperienced and overwhelmed by adult problems, to feel her mother's arms around her and smell the sweet perfume her mother wore, to have her mother get a damp cloth for her forehead and tell her everything was going to be all right. "Time for me to be the one who's lost in the wilderness, huh?" she said, referring to the old joke they shared about the flock of one hundred.

"Tell me," Mrs. Lovejoy coaxed.

Charity did, and concluded with, "He's been hurt so badly that he's terrified of commitment. Maybe he'd have been able to get over a broken marriage, but he also lost his child, and he blames himself. I don't think he'll ever let himself be happy. He has to punish himself. So you see, it's hopeless."

"What makes you so sure it's hopeless?" Mrs. Lovejoy said.

"It just is," Charity said. "He's been hurt too badly."

"Charity, didn't you learn anything at all growing up in this household?"

Taken aback by her mother's impatient tone, Charity said, "What do you mean?"

"Didn't you say you loved him?"

"Yes, but—"

"Don't give me excuses. Does he care about you—do you think he might love you if he weren't hurting so badly over his previous marriage and losing his child?"

"Yes, but—"

"Charity, what is the only antidote for the pain that humans are capable of feeling?"

"Love?" Charity said. So many times she'd heard her father or mother say, "When people are hurting, the only antidote we can give them is love."

"The question, as I see it, is whether or not you love him enough to help him through the pain."

"I'm not sure he wants my love."

"He may not be ready to give up the pain yet," Mrs. Lovejoy replied, "but everyone wants to be loved."

"Lance doesn't," Charity said.

"Are you so sure of that?"

Charity sighed wearily. She wasn't sure of anything anymore.

"Sometimes," Mrs. Lovejoy said, "the people who need love the most resist it the most vehemently."

"A person can't just shove love down someone's throat," Charity said. "It wouldn't work with Lance."

"Well, you know the situation better than I do," Mrs. Lovejoy said. "Anyway, you're a smart girl, and I know you'll work it all out. Why don't you get out of bed and go shop for a birthday present for your brother and take yourself out for a nice lunch. You'll feel better."

Charity found the phone call, the advice, unsettling. If there was one thing on which she prided herself in this whole disgusting mess into which she'd gotten herself mired, it was her acceptance of the fact that Lance did not want a permanent relationship. She accepted the hopelessness of the situation with a fortitude her mother hadn't seemed to notice.

She took a long, hot shower, hoping the water would clear the cobwebs out of her brain. Then she followed her mother's advice and went shopping. It was a therapeutic excursion, and Charity allowed herself to get lost in the press of the Saturday mall crowds as she picked out a challenging jigsaw puzzle and a sport shirt for her brother and selected a new pair of slippers to replace her worn satin scuffs.

In the card shop, she stopped to browse at the display of contemporary graffiti printed on cards suitable for posting in offices. She recognized old standards like, "I never make a missteak," or "An orderly desk is a sign of a sick mind," and chuckled over some of the newer expressions on frustration, discontent and independence. One in particular caught her attention. She'd seen it before but never found it particularly relevant or inspiring. *It's hard to soar like an eagle when you're dealing with turkeys.*

She read the epigram and reread it, wondering why it seemed to be reaching out and grabbing her by the lapels. She wasn't dealing with any turkeys she could think of. It wasn't until later, after she'd paid for her brother's birthday card and was standing in the lunch-hour line at Morrison's Cafeteria that a realization came to her: she wasn't dealing with turkeys, she was the turkey the other eagles were trying to deal with. She was the one flapping her wings a couple of feet off the ground. An eagle like Lance couldn't be expected to go flying with a turkey.

She hardly tasted her lunch in her impatience to get back to the stores. She had a lot of shopping to do. There were things eagles needed that turkeys never dreamed of. Mentally, she listed the items she'd need and the stores that would carry them. First the lingerie store, then the drug store....

"Wanna clean them here or take them back to your place?" Eddie asked.

"Clean them here," Lance said. He bobbed his head toward the end of the pier. "The pelicans will eat the heads."

Agent Double-O-Fishbreath was perched in his favorite spot, watching them, constantly reminding Lance of Charity. Not that he didn't miss her at other times, too—like every time he opened the refrigerator and thought of the salmonella lurking in hidden recesses, or when Tilly sat at his feet and looked at him as if to ask where the nice lady who used to scratch him behind the ears had gone, or when he used his iron skillet and remembered how encrusted it had become when he'd cooked the redfish Charity'd caught.

He missed her when he worked, too. He was halfway through the chapter he was supposed to be writing for the next week, but charting the adventures of Shea and Erskine simply wasn't as much fun without Charity around, debating over some passage of dialogue or bantering about Erskine's chauvinistic attitude.

He wondered what she had decided about the sequel. Tony would have called him if she'd settled the matter one way or the other, but it was requiring extraordinary willpower on his behalf not to call her and ask what she was thinking, which way she was leaning.

He even, at odd moments, was tempted to call her and say, "I'm scared to death of hurting you, but I'm even more terrified of losing you." But he couldn't do that when their personal lives were so linked to their professional ones. She alone had to make the decision about whether or not to continue working with him, just as he needed to decide how far he was willing to go for her. Though he was beginning to think it could work between them, he wasn't quite ready to believe in the happily-ever-after ending she was dreaming of. He was ready to make room for her in his life, but not quite ready to promise her wedding bells and baby buggies.

"Hey, partner, you going to clean fish or sit there looking at that stupid pelican?" Eddie said.

"That's not a stupid pelican," Lance said. "It's Agent Double-O-Fishbreath, undercover spy for the Tony Tyson Literary Agency."

"Why the hell don't you just call Charity and get it over with?" Eddie said. "You're flipping out."

Lance ground his fists into his waist. "What makes you think my flipping out has anything to do with Charity Lovejoy?"

"Oh, nothing much. Except your surliness, your foul mood, the homicidal gleam in your eye every time her name is mentioned. Jeez, Lance, this is your old partner you're talking to. I went through the labor pains of love with you when you were courting Katy."

Lance frowned. "You could have gone all day without mentioning Katy. I wish you had." He didn't want to be reminded of failure when he was entertaining the possibility of success.

"She's history, Lance. Let her go. What happened happened, but you can't let the past screw up your future. I loved Wanda, too, but nothing's going to bring back yesterday."

"You and Wanda didn't have a kid."

"All right, Lance. You win the bad break award. It's harder for you. There's more to forget. Only you don't really have to forget Bobby, you know. He's still yours. The best is yet to come with him. He'll be old enough for visits in another couple of years."

"I missed all the best times. His walking and talking and his first tooth."

"Look, Lance, you can't change that. Putting on a hair shirt and holing up here in the middle of nowhere and living like a monk is not going to get those days back for you. It wouldn't be disloyal to Bobby or Katy for you to settle down with Charity and have babies."

Lance slashed into the fish he was cleaning rather savagely and, nicking his finger with the sharp knife, uttered a blistering curse.

"Distracted?" Eddie said, amused.

"Did anyone ever tell you that you talk too much?" Lance grumbled.

"The last time was just before I graduated from the police academy." He tossed the head of the fish he'd just cleaned to Double-O-Fishbreath. "That was about the time you were working up your courage to propose to Katy, wasn't it?"

The next time either of them spoke was when they were back at Lance's house. "Want to fry up the day's catch for dinner?" Lance said.

"Not tonight. I'm supposed to meet a couple of guys at Antonio's to watch the basketball game."

They both knew it was an excuse, but Lance didn't argue. He'd had enough of Eddie's candor for one day.

"Hey, thanks for printing out my letters on your computer," Eddie said. "That's neat. Just type in a new address, press a few buttons and, bingo! an original letter. And thanks for the letter of recommendation."

"What are partners for?" Lance said blithely.

"Partners tell it like it is," Eddie said. He looked at his key chain, singled out the key to his ignition, then looked back at Lance. "You know, all that stuff I said about putting the past behind you wasn't do-as-I-say-and-not-as-I-do. I'm putting the whole lousy mess with Tampa P.D. behind me with these letters. It feels good, Lance. Really good. Maybe that's why I'm on a soap-box. No hard feelings?"

"No hard feelings," Lance said.

He had showered and changed clothes and was just trying to decide whether he really wanted to go to the trouble to fry fish for dinner when Charity soared up to his front porch and rang the doorbell. Wondering if Eddie had forgotten something, he followed Tilly to the door. Surprise registered on his face when he saw Charity standing there with a suitcase in one hand and a cat carrier in the other.

While he was waiting for his power of speech to return, Tilly was expressing violent objections to having a cat invade his territory. Springing into action, Lance pulled back on Tilly's collar. "Down, boy. Calm down."

"I guess it's going to take a while for them to get used to each other," Charity said.

"Come in," Lance said stiffly, like a schoolboy just remembering his manners. "I'll put Tilly out on the deck for a while." When he returned, Charity had moved her baggage inside and closed the door.

For several seconds they stared at each other, their eyes asking questions too comprehensive for words. Charity was the first to speak. "I called Tony today. I said we'd do the sequel."

"I'm glad," Lance said softly.

"So am I."

A silence stretched between them, so intense that it seemed like a living presence in the small room.

Finally, Lance succumbed to suspense. "Charity?" he asked, and all the pertinent questions were contained in the simple speaking of her name.

Charity sucked in a fortifying breath and said, "Please listen to me and don't say anything until I'm finished because if I stop, I'm afraid I'll lose my nerve and go bolting out the door like a turkey, and I've been a stupid turkey as long as I'm going to be."

Lance nodded, and she continued. "First, I want you to know that I'm here for as long as you want me here, but I'll leave any time you ask me to—five minutes from now or five years from now. I've brought enough clothes for a few days, but I'll have to go back to my place periodically to get more and check the mail, so you won't have to worry about asking me to leave because I'll still have my apartment anytime I need it."

She took another breath. "I want you to know that I love you, and nothing I want has changed, but I understand completely that you aren't ready for any long-term commitment and I'm willing to live with that because I have a lot of faith in you and the type of person you are. You're afraid now, afraid of hurting me or being hurt, but that's okay, because sooner or later you're going to realize that I'm not Katy. I'm not clinging or dependent the way she was, and I won't make unrealistic demands, and you're not an immature kid anymore, trying to prove you're super cop, so you're going to be a lot more sensitive to my needs than you were to Katy's.

"Finally, I want to say I'm sorry for making you feel guilty because you didn't want the things I wanted. The fact is I've been blind. I fell in love with a perfectly wonderful flesh-and-blood man and then tried to turn him into some paper hero from one of my books. But now I know you couldn't be a hero for me because I wasn't much of a heroine for you. I was timid and unreasonable and judgmental and everything else a heroine is not supposed to be. But I'm not any of those things anymore. I'm scared to death, but that's okay, because I suspect you're probably just as scared as I am and for all the same reasons. I just want to say I love you just the way you are, and I'm willing to take a chance on your eventually loving me.''

He was staring at her, his face unreadable, and when she couldn't bear the silence anymore, she said, ''Now you can ask me to leave, or tell me I'm crazy, or put your arms around me and kiss me like you're glad to see me. And while I'd prefer that you kiss me, I'll understa—''

The expression in his eyes stopped her in midword as he lifted his hand to cup her cheek in his fingertips.

''I love you,'' he said, his voice filled with awe.

Charity had never felt anything so sensuous as the way his fingers feathered over the soft skin of her cheek. ''You don't have to say that,'' she said, without conviction.

Lance seemed not to hear her, and plunged his arms around her and hugged her body against his urgently. ''I want you,'' he said. ''I *need* you. God, Charity, I'm glad you're here.''

His face lowered to hers slowly, and his lips hovered just above hers for an infinity of seconds before finally claiming them. Charity thought fleetingly that the reality of Lance Palmer was better than any hero she could have created on paper. But the thought, like all others, fled from her mind as she quit thinking and started reacting the way any respectable heroine reacted when the man of her dreams was kissing her.

Epilogue

Charity leveled an exasperated glare at Tony. "Not today, Tony. You promised."

"One little reporter," he said, unintimidated. "It's the Associated Press, sweetheart. No telling how many feature sections you'd hit. We couldn't buy publicity like this for an arm and a leg."

"I have a feeling you'd try, if you thought it was possible," Charity replied dryly.

"Look," Tony said. "All you have to do is look at the camera and smile, and you're already smiling. I just saw Lance, and he's smiling, too. So what's it going to cost you to flash that smile in front of a camera?"

Charity laughed and pressed a kiss on his cheek. "Okay, Tony. You win. I'm not letting anything spoil today. The photographer can stay."

Tony opened his mouth to speak, but Charity cut him off. "He can take any pictures he likes—but *after* the ceremony."

The photograph of Charity and Lance being congratulated by their literary agent, Tony Tyson, appeared in over a hundred newspapers across the country. Many a features editor selected it for its poignant depiction of a happy couple: bride in white lace, groom in tuxedo and ascot, both smiling broadly. The groom's arm was around the bride, and his left hand rested possessively on her trim waist as he shook hands with a spiffily dressed wedding guest.

The caption below the photograph identified the couple, mentioned their best-selling novel *The Carlotta Chronicles* and noted that the bride's father, the Reverend Mark Thomas Lovejoy, officiated at the ceremony.

No note was made of the conversation between bride and groom that immediately preceded the snapping of the photograph.

"Was the formal wedding as awful as you were afraid it would be?" Charity whispered.

"It's not awful at all," Lance whispered back. "But—"

Their eyes met. "But what?" Charity asked.

"I'll be glad when it's over so we can be alone, *Mrs. Palmer.*"

Charity pressed as close to him as propriety and the full skirt of her dress would permit. "So will I, Mr. Palmer. So will I."

* * * * *

Silhouette Romance

COMING NEXT MONTH

#568 JACINTH—Laurey Bright
Lovely Jacinth Norwood wouldn't let a man inside her secret world, but Mark Harding knew he belonged there. His passion for her was growing—could it melt her icy shell?

#569 THE TAKEOVER MAN—Frances Lloyd
When she bumped into the new director of promotion, advertising executive Kate Camilleri thought she'd never met a more infuriating man—or a more handsome one. Nick Wedderburn's charm might burn her in the end, but Kate didn't care—he could set her heart on fire....

#570 A HALF-DOZEN REASONS—Darlene Patten
Grant Russell was what Karen Wagner had always wanted—affectionate, funny and powerfully attractive. But he was the father of six children! Karen had never seen herself as Maria von Trapp, but she'd climb every mountain to find her dream with Grant.

#571 SOMEDAY MY LOVE—Patti Beckman
When Dak Roberts left town to become an Olympic star, he vowed he'd return to Kathy Ayers someday. That day had come—Dak looked at Kathy and knew, for the first time in his life, he was really home....

#572 POPCORN AND KISSES—Kasey Michaels
Theater manager Sharon Wheeler loved the romance of the old drive-in, but Zachary St. Clair, head of the corporation, thought she was living in the past. He was profits and losses while she was popcorn and kisses. Would the future bring them together?

#573 BABY MAKES THREE—Sharon De Vita
What could be better than a man who'd won a Mother of the Year award? Maggie Magee had never thought about it—until she met "Wild Bill" Cody and his little son, Bobby. Now Maggie wanted to win the greatest prize of all—Cody's heart.

AVAILABLE THIS MONTH:

ATTRACTIVE, SPACE SAVING BOOK RACK

Display your most prized novels on this handsome and sturdy book rack. The hand-rubbed walnut finish will blend into your library decor with quiet elegance, providing a practical organizer for your favorite hard-or soft-covered books.

Only $9.95

Approximately 16" x 8" when assembled

Assembles in seconds!

To order, rush your name, address and zip code, along with a check or money order for $10.70* ($9.95 plus 75¢ postage and handling) payable to *Silhouette Books.*

Silhouette Books
Book Rack Offer
901 Fuhrmann Blvd.
P.O. Box 1396
Buffalo, NY 14269-1396

Offer not available in Canada.

BKR-2A

*New York and Iowa residents add appropriate sales tax.

Silhouette Romance™

Legendary Lovers Trilogy

BY DEBBIE MACOMBER....

ONCE UPON A TIME, in a land not so far away, there lived a girl, Debbie Macomber, who grew up dreaming of castles, white knights and princes on fiery steeds. Her family was an ordinary one with a mother and father and one wicked brother, who sold copies of her diary to all the boys in her junior high class.

One day, when Debbie was only nineteen, a handsome electrician drove by in a shiny black convertible. Now Debbie knew a prince when she saw one, and before long they lived in a two-bedroom cottage surrounded by a white picket fence.

As often happens when a damsel fair meets her prince charming, children followed, and soon the two-bedroom cottage became a four-bedroom castle. The kingdom flourished and prospered, and between soccer games and car pools, ballet classes and clarinet lessons, Debbie thought about love and enchantment and the magic of romance.

One day Debbie said, "What this country needs is a good fairy tale." She remembered how well her diary had sold and she dreamed again of castles, white knights and princes on fiery steeds. And so the stories of Cinderella, Beauty and the Beast, and Snow White were reborn....

Look for Debbie Macomber's *Legendary Lovers* trilogy from Silhouette Romance: *Cindy and the Prince* (January, 1988); *Some Kind of Wonderful* (March, 1988); *Almost Paradise* (May, 1988). Don't miss them!

SRT-1